I DON'T DO DIVORCE CASES

David Justice

I0684895

Lingua Sacra Publishing

I Don't Do Divorce Cases
Copyright © 2009 by David Justice

Published in the United States by Lingua Sacra
Publishing.
www.linguasacrapublishing.com
ISBN 978-0-9843432-2-5

Dedication

To my wife.

Acknowledgements

With warm appreciation for my friend Keith who
revived these stories from the drawer wherein they'd
slumbered —

new life for dry bones...

About the Author

David Justice, Ph.D., is the author of *The Semantics of
Form in Arabic.* He was editor of Etymology and
Pronunciation at Merriam-Webster, and Editor-in-
Chief at Franklin Electronic Publishers. His short
stories have appeared in *Ellery Queen* and *Alfred
Hitchcock's Mystery Magazine.* He is currently
working as a linguist.

I Don't Do Divorce Cases

SHORT STORIES

META-MURPHY

UPCOMING NOVELS

VALEDICTION

NICE KNOWING YOU

[Originally published as: "I Don't Do Divorce Cases" in *Ellery Queen*, November 1987.]

When he come through the door, I don't know is he on the level or out to lunch. He looks around, he looks around some more, then he looks straight at me. He says he wants me to locate this dame who's gone missing. Okay, fine, but then he gives me an address where I'll find her at ten o'clock that night. I say I don't do divorce cases — I say that just to have something to say while I'm figuring what his game is. He says he isn't married to her and he isn't related to her. He just wants me to find her and learn everything I can about her. I figure the guy's a fruitcake, but he flashes a roll of bills at me and I figure my diet can stand some fruit. He's on, at twice the going rate.

Does this dame have a name? I begin, smiling. She does, but you don't need to know it yet, he says. Wants my first impressions to be free of associations. Great. How will I recognize her? He gives me a photograph, black and white, a little blurry, says, Memorize it, then burn it. No kidding, that's what he says. And I must admit she is one good-looking dame. Early twenties, but not so early there's any problem with the law. Dark haired. Eyes a little out of focus or maybe it's the camera. Then he thinks better of it and snatches it back, says I've seen enough. He's right, I have. Maybe he figures I wouldn't burn it. He's right, I wouldn't.

The address turns out to be a loft in an artsy part of the city. I show up a little early. I figure it'll be a little strange, me just bursting in on her, but there's no problem. The room is huge, there's some sort of party going on. Already lots of bodies and I just walk in real confident and nobody challenges. The blonde who opened the door wasn't doing it for me, anyway — she was just leaving the party to shoot up or be sick.

I'm dressed like a P.I. It doesn't matter. I don't exactly fit right in, but in this zoo I don't stick out. You got people dressed like Philip Marlowe, you got people dressed like Tarzan — before the party's over, you got people that they're not dressed at all.

Lots of bodies and some not bad broads, some of which are probably really men. No sign of the little lady. I grab a drink and wait.

Ten o'clock comes on and in walks the hot property. Right, you couldn't mistake her, but even so that snapshot oughta be shot for treason. Good-looking and what she is are just different ballparks. It's like trying to photograph a waterfall, or a moving cloud. Murphy, you're getting sloppy, but I mean really. Less and less am I blaming the guy.

This first trip, he said, no specifics. Just a general idea of what she drinks and who she talks to. And I'm supposed to get a bead on what she's really like. I watch, she doesn't see me watching her. At eleven, she leaves alone.

I meet my party at midnight in the diner like he said. He is sitting at a table alone, smoking. Cup of coffee, untouched. He is, how do I say it, unsentimental, He gives me these narrow eyes.

"Well?"

I tell him all I know about her. "Drinks plain vermouth, not a whole lot of it. Seems to know everyone, but only talks to a few. One guy in particular seemed interested but she wasn't interested back. She left alone."

"Did you follow her?"

"You didn't tell me to."

He relaxes a little. "Good, good. I like your action, Murphy. Here's for tonight."

He rounds it off, upwards. Then he gives me another address for tomorrow, mid-afternoon …

He might've said what it was, save me going around peering at all these street numbers where half the joints don't have any. Turns out it's the public library, f'r cr'sakes. I go in, this time feeling really out of place. I start browsing, so-called. Then I notice what I'm browsing — Young Adult Romance — and move off in disgust. I grab a novel off the shelves and make like I'm reading it. In she comes.

Now she's, dressed simple, but she's even more beautiful that way. Even better without makeup — anyhow, 'none I can detect. (Not that I know a damn thing about it.) She moves easily through the rows of books. Her slender hand selects a volume. A sad smile plays on her lips and, oh, Murphy, now you're talking like one. Just stay professional, you're not hitched up with this girl.

She settles on something and goes to the circulation desk. I go up behind her with whatever it is I've got and I get a gander at what she's checking out. Something about a swan in love. Sounds kinky, but this isn't the kind of place to carry anything like that. As she heads for the door, I hand the librarian my book and gaze, gaze after her. I'm not supposed to follow her, but I stand at the glass doors and watch her go tripping down the steps and out of my life forever, oh, Murphy, oh Murphy, you've got it bad. But I don't go anywhere because I don't have a card. I'm stuck at the counter, feeling like a fool, and the librarian is very nice and says it's all right, will I just give my name and address and they can let me have the book on a temporary card. I mean, how decent is that? But there's no *time*, there's just no *time* ... She says: Please allow two weeks for the permanent replacement but I'm like, oh lady, oh lady, thank you and bless you but: gotta go now; gotta go put coins in the meter; I left the *burner* on, left the *water* running, gotta run, okay? Gotta — gotta go see a fella about a dog.

I meet him at a luncheonette. This time he pays me before I even report. When he hears about the swan book, he gets real excited and says, Yes, that's just exactly right, things are going perfectly. Then he gives me another address for that very night.

I say, You seem to know a lot about this dame, always knowing where she's going to be. Not always, he says sternly, and there's a lot he doesn't know.

That night turns out to be the theater. Maybe he saw her buy tickets, there's some good explanation. Anyhow, he has one for me in the row behind her. I watch the actors. The play is hard to follow, but I watch her responses. It goes on like this all evening. Lots and lots of reaction shots, only shot from behind.

I meet him at a deli near the theater. "What can I tell you? She liked the play."

He seemed pleased. "She has good taste." Then he surprises me and asks if I liked it.

"Umm ... Refresh my memory. What play was it?" I ask him.

Again he seems pleased ...

The next day I follow her shopping, writing down everything she buys. After that it's an art museum. I'm supposed to say how long she spends at each painting, does she talk to anyone, does she look at any of them twice.

He studies the purchase list, frowning, but clears up when I tell him she charged it. I'm guessing maybe she's getting in over her head and could use his dough. She spent different times at different paintings, and let me tell you it was a pain going back and getting all the names.

No, she didn't talk to anyone, just to ask the guard something, like maybe where's the bathroom. Yes, she did go back to this one painting. What was it? Just a bunch of nothing, I say, the title claimed water lilies, you could have fooled me. His head tilts back and he kisses his own fingers, blows the kiss out into space.

Somehow this gets to me and I say, if you're so keen on her why don't *you* follow her?

He comes back to earth fast and starts frowning and says, You don't ask the questions — but the way he says it I can see he's shaken and I figure he's really just a little afraid of her. If you weren't just paid to do it, just a job, and you really really wanted her, I can see where a guy would freeze up.

Only then I get another idea and I'm thinking how he's maybe some kind of pervert and he really wants to bump her off. Only why would he want to do that? Anyhow, just keep your mitts off her, I almost say.

He glowers at me and I glower at him and he hands me another address, but I say I'm busy that day. Oh, you're busy that day, are you — real sarcastic, but he doesn't press the point. Okay, meet me at such and such a place at 10:00 P.M., anyway, and he'll have a different address. Okay.

I got back to my apartment and shower and have a TV dinner and don't finish it. I can't get the address out of my mind. I lay awake a while and then decide I'm going there, anyway. I fall asleep eventually. Crazy dreams.

It's a kind of stadium, next to the middle of nowhere. Weeds are growing up through the marble and you can tell it was really something once, but they must of screwed up because it's coming apart now, in bits and pieces, here and there. She walks slowly around the high part of it and I stand watching her and not moving. If she sees me, she doesn't show it. Then she leaves ...

That night at the diner, he gives the narrow-eye treatment and I'm gruff so as not to be nervous. He hands me an address and says, Don't try to pull anything. I tell him he minds his business and I mind mine. He says *that's* a laugh, and it is, it's a laugh and a half, because I'm minding *her* business and he's buying *mine*.

This time it's a restaurant. Fancy place, but she's dining alone. I take a table not far from her. Not professional, Murphy, you could've seen her just as good from across the room.

She has a glass of wine and a cheese plate, then some kind of mixed-up stuff that I don't know its name. Bad luck — I already got my steak or I could've said *I'll have what the lady is having* and found out. Anyway, she has water with it, then salad, then some green stuff in a little glass.

I go to the drop and just read out the menu in a bored voice like a sergeant who for some reason he's a short-order cook. Wine, cheese, some French thing, water, salad. I stop. He waits. He looks at me. Well?

Well what? How about my dollars?

The man is not buying it. *You're holding out on me*, he says.

Like splat I'm holding out on you. Don't gimme that. She didn't see anyone. I didn't talk with her. Whachoo looking at me that way for?

You haven't told me everything.

Yes, I did. Everything. She just sat alone, all by herself, and ate, not much, and not much wine at all. One glass, plus a glass of some greenish stuff.

Some greenish stuff, he says, very polite. I'm ready to bust him if he's getting sarcastic, but now he relaxes. *Absinthe*, he murmurs like he's talking to himself. He gets this far-off look. I say, What gives? He comes back to our planet and he pays me, he actually smiles.

He gives me an address for nine o'clock at night. It's just a sidewalk in front of a record store that's closed. A traffic light, going through the motions — hardly any traffic. An alleyway with garbage cans. But this time the stakes are higher: he's told me to close in, to get closer, let her see me.

And she shows up, all right. She comes across the street and mails a letter. I step out of the shadows. She puts her hand to her mouth, stifles a scream. I put my hands out, palms forward, like, Lady, don't blame me. She speaks for the first time I hear her really speak clearly. "*What have you been following me for*?"

And, damn, I just don't have an answer. My mouth opens but nothing comes out. I move toward her. My head I think it's going from side to side, the mouth is moving but the mind is reeling, and ... She steps backward, looking afraid.

And then the guy shows up, Mr. Mystery Employer. She looks at him and my jaw drops, because she's only a little bit surprised and now she's less scared. "Why, *Charles*, what are you doing here?"

He smiles, really debonair, and takes her hand.

"This man has been following me," she says, and she points at me.

I'm a big guy but it stops me dead in my tracks.

"Oh, he has, has he?"

He turns on me and he's about six inches shorter and has this topcoat on and he's not in condition like I am, but he's got me where he wants me and he's a lot better shaved.

In an even, steely voice, every word perfect, like he's imagined this speech for a long time: "I catch you around this lady again and I'll clean the pavement with you, you understand? Don't let me see your face again in this town ever, never. You got a gun in that trench coat I could care less. Guys like you I have for breakfast and spit out the bones. Now beat it."

Now I'm walking backward and my mouth is moving, but nothing's coming down from the brain. Then I turn, I'm stumbling, genuinely at a loss, choking back a sob, really, and I start cursing myself under my breath and walk back to the subway, hopelessly defeated, through the gathering dark. The last thing I hear him say is: "Come on, darling, I'll take you home."

The next day I get a check in the mail for my time plus a goodbye sweetener. He signs off wishing me the best of luck. That's the last I ever saw of him.

~ *The End* ~

Murphy Considers his Sins

Man, I really tied one on last night. Might've done some things I'll be sorry for later. Only, how can I be sorry if I don't remember what I did? Jeez, I better write this stuff down.

Lingua Sacra is pleased to announce the following series of volumes, written by Mr. Michael Murphy, and edited by a prestigious ivy-league type with a Ph.D. after his name:

My Sins, by Murphy.
Volume I: The Early Years.
Volume VIII: That Time in Chicago.
Volume XXVII: Just Last Week.

DON'T MENTION IT

[First appeared in *Alfred Hitchcock's Mystery Magazine*, May 1988]

So one time, another time, musta been 'bout April, we're sittin' around, thinking: maybe play some pool. But Joey says no, too nice a day, and we go out to the sidewalk looking at the old cars, the new cars, and the garbage cans. Then up off in the distance, sort of shimmering in the smog, Joey spots this dame.

"She's heading our way," notes Joey.

"Ye-es, she's coming on down the line."

"This could be a customer coming in."

"Could right sure be one at that."

Now, fact a the matter, we do this a lot, pass the time; but this one time, this one dame, she didn't turn down a side street or keep right on walking by, just kept heading straight for us; so this is the time I'm telling you about.

She keeps walking towards us like she's coming into focus. Joey and I stop what we're saying and just watch. When she gets right up to us, she stops.

'I'm looking for ..."

"You found it," I say.

She nods. We go into the building and head upstairs.

She looks to be about forty, made up to look younger. Pretty clothes, but frayed. She sees the sign that says MURPHY BROS. PRIVATE INVESTIGATORS and says, kind of archly, "You are the brothers Murphy?"

"Yeh, I'm Murphy, and he's Joey," I say.

She frowns.

I push open the door. The office, unfortunately, is just like we left it. Crud all over everything. Moose head in the sink.

"Have a seat," I say gravely, indicating an overturned crate. She looks around doubtfully. "Is this where you work?"

"Well, the penthouse suite is being renovated, so for right now — yes. This is where I work. And eat, and sleep, and — right behind that door there — play pool. So, state your business."

"I — I — I don't know quite how to say this — "

"It's all right, we know. Your husband disappeared."

She looks at me with a round mouth. "How did you know?"

"We're detectives, lady, remember? Look, it happens alla time. Only kinda case we get, really." I look over at Joey and he gives a helpless shrug.

"Oh! Then I have indeed come to the right place. You are — specialists, then?"

"Y'might say, y'might say."

She nods, with furrowed brow. "Then I am in your hands."

"So!" I say, happy to have a case at last. "When did your husband disappear?"

She speaks quite distinctly, as though saying a set piece. "Precisely one year ago today."

I look over at Joey and notice he's lookin' at me. We both got the same look.

"Uh — lady … you ever report this to the police?"

"I did not. They could not possibly understand."

"Hmm, okay. And, why did you wait to come to us until, ah, one year to the day?"

"I believe in anniversaries," she said primly. "This is also, I might mention, the fifteenth anniversary of our having met."

"Oh, well, many happy returns of the day. Sort of. Now, your name?"

Again quite distinctly, "Mrs. Roger Bosworth."

I hate it when dames do that. I mean, they got a name, don't they? The "Mrs." already tells you they're hitched. "Mrs. Roger Bosworth" sounds like Roger Bosworth in drag.

"Okay, ah, maiden name?"

"As a maiden," she says, "I was known as Vera Simms." Somehow this doesn't sound quite right.

"Okay. Now, usually, we like ta have the clients come in a little earlier, 'cause the circumstances of the disappearance can give us clues."

"I remember it as clearly as though it were today."

"Uh — oh, good. Well. So. Describe it. If you would be so good."

Her eyes got a faraway look.

"It was a melancholy day in April, a day much like today. The evening settled early. We had been to a matinee — the sort of brittle thing the theater thrives on, then throws away.

"We returned to our home in the country. The servants had gone out. I sat upon the window seat, gazing across the vast expanse of lawn. Roger had put on his dressing gown and had gone to the den to mix drinks. When he did not return, I became disturbed. Fear, or some nameless emotion, seized and held my breast."

I let out a low whistle. "I shoulda made popcorn." She went on like she didn't notice.

"I went to the den; he was not there. A decanter of fine gin stood on a sideboard, with no glass or ice or tonic. It was then that I began to suspect that something had gone wrong.

"I fled to the bedroom, the study — the patio and the salon. I even inspected the kitchen. But my husband, my lover, was gone!

"And when I returned to the windows, I found on the mantel — this note."

She reached into her bosom — my eyes followed her fingers all the way down — and drew out a pale blue sheet of paper. "You may read."

I took it, not liking the setup too much. "Dearest treasure," it said, "my life, my light, I — " and then it broke off. Written in a florid, almost feminine hand.

I'm not liking this. My brain has come to a complete stop. I want to somehow back up. But Joey plows right in.

"I don't get it. Yer sittin' right next to these winders, in the, what room now — ?"

She looks flustered. "The — the drawing room."

"Yeh right, the drawn room. An'en, you go in ta where this guy — sorry, yer husband — is whomping up some booze."

She shivers, and nods.

"To the what you call it, the den."

A quick nod, as though wanting to get this over with.

"An'en it looks like he disappears right from there, right? Am I followin'? Cos he just got the gin wit'out none a the fixin's. Course, that's the way *I* drink it, but I get the idea yer old man liked limes in it, and spritz in it, and maybe little flags. Okay. So, bingo, somethin' innarupted 'im. An'en you go haulin' out after 'im, an'—"

"Please, Mr. Murphy."

"Call me Joey. An'en'e's not there, an' you mess aroun', mess aroun', an'en you go back and, double bingo, there's a note, right? what ain't been there before?"

"I — I couldn't say."

"'Cos like you don't meet him onna way. It's just — I mean are there like two entrances to this den and this, like, drawing room? Like in a Marx brothers? Or are we

17

dealin' here with one a them *locked-room* jobs — just one entrance, under strict surveillance, no windows — but maybe a chimney. Right! A chimney! Was there like a fireplace in this den? I mean — "

"It's difficult to explain."

"Yeh, I kin see that. Maybe it'd help if we could see the house."

"I'm ... afraid that won't be possible. We had to sell the estate. The creditors were relentless. Since that day I have had no support, a widow in all but name. At present I am residing in an apartment."

"How long you been there, ma'am?" I ask.

"I beg your — ? Oh. Let me see. Well, it would be three years."

"Maybe exactly three years, like an anniversary?"

"No," she says, a little frostily.

"All right," I say, "forget the floor plan. You heard anything from him since then?"

Again the knitted brow. "Not from Roger personally, no. But about a year after his disappearance, I received an envelope with no return address, postmarked from the south of France. It said: 'Abandon your futile efforts to learn the truth.' The truth of what, it did not specify."

I'm liking this less and less and less.

"All right, ahh, look. Can you tell us the name of any of his associates, any places he went regular, stuff like that?"

"Certainly. He was a member of the Nautical Club, here in town.

And of the Belmont, of course."

"The Belmont?"

"The country club, just outside the city limits."

"Yeh, okay. Friends?"

"Of course he had friends! Dozens and dozens of them!"

"Mm-right ... Names?"

She frowned. "That — I cannot give you. He was ... there was always an air of mystery about his work."

"Oof, you ain't makin' this easy. Okay, your address, and a number you can be reached."

"I am at Apartment 3B, Bellerose Terrace apartments, 1898 Eighth Street. The phone is 757-1171." I nod, and slap my pocket.

"Hey, Joey, you got a pencil there, pal?"

Joey frowns and looks down at his T-shirt. No pocket. So, no place to put a pencil. He reaches for his trousers pocket, but can't get his hand in, so he stands up, plunges both hands down, and comes up empty. He's starting to sit down when he thinks of something, straightens up, puts both hands in his back trousers pockets, and comes up with a wad of stuff but no pencil. Then he puts it back, thinks, shakes his head, and sits down. I'm gritting my teeth.

"Sorry, Murphy, no pencil. You got one?"

"Joey, would I ask you for a pencil if I got one myself?"

19

"I dunno, Murphy, you do strange things."

"Yeh, tell me about it. Excuse me, Mrs. Bosworth, do you by any chance have a pencil I might borrow?"

"I — I don't know." She looks reluctantly at her handbag, a little narrow job looks more like a pencil case than anything, but I guess she got more important things in there than pencils. She opens it, rummages, rummages some more, and some stuff spills out. I pick it up — lipstick and the like — but in among it I notice a library card, the city library.

Now, normally, when I know something someone else don't know, I like to keep it private, 'cause it puts me one up. But in this case the only thing is that she don't know I know it, and I'm more interested in what she will say.

"Mrs. Bosworth, I notice that your library card is made out to 'Vera Simms'. Any special reason?"

"Yes, yes I, I went back to using it after my husband disappeared, that is, after it looked, it seemed as if he would not be coming back."

"I see. One final thing. Where did your husband go to college?"

"Why do you ask?"

"Well, you know, it might give us a lead. You know, the old school tie."

"Princeton," she said proudly, with a small smile and a lift of her head.

I call the Princeton records office and it's like I figured: no record. I head over the city library and go through the past twenty years' phone books. Some years there's a V. Simms, some years nothing, but never any Bosworth, Roger, Mr. and Mrs.

Joey comes back from checking out the leads, all hot and bothered.

"I don't believe it, Murphy, this case is deeper than I thought. This guy has vanished without a trace. No trace after — no trace before! The country club's got nothing, and nothing at the Nautical, neither. Someone musta got in and rifled their records. Not in the archives, and nobody admits he knows him. Somebody's scared, Murph. If ya ask me, it's a innernational gang."

"Yeh, thanks, Joey, could be. Look, you wait here, I'm gonna check in with Mrs. Bosworth, straighten out a few points."

I leave him puzzling over these notes he's written up.

The first thing I want to straighten is this damn dame's head. She's been holding out on me, playing me for a chump. I don't like that in a client.

I head over to Eighth Street — not a real great address — and realize I've forgotten the house number, what I never written down. But the "Bellerose Terrace" sticks in my mind, one a these phony fancy names like a window box with plastic flowers. I find it, and head up to Apartment 3A.

A little old lady answers. She smiles — either trusting, or just too old to be afraid. She invites me in.

"Hello ma'am, sorry to bother you. My name is Michael Murphy. Is ah, is Mrs., is Vera Bosworth in?"

"No one's in but me, ever. I live alone."

"I — oh. You're not the mother, or a housekeeper, or ..."

"I am a mother, but not 'the' mother, whatever that may mean."

"See, I'm looking for a Mrs. Roger Bosworth. Also goes by the name of Vera Simms."

"Oh yes, Vera lives just across the landing, in 3B."

"Oh, I'm sorry, I come to the wrong apartment." But I'm not sorry. This grandma looks like she lived here a long time. Sixty years' worth a photos and stuff on the walls, anyway.

"Tell me, you know Mrs. Bosworth a long time?"

"I don't know a Mrs. Bosworth. You mean Vera, yes?"

"Yes."

"I have lived in this apartment for fifteen years. She has been here about five."

"Five — not three. You're certain."

"Certainly I'm certain. Before that there was that horrible man."

"Is Vera married?"

"Mr. Murphy, such questions you ask."

"I'm sorry. Look, Mrs. —"

"Rieger."

"Mrs. Rieger. I'm a detective. Vera hired me to find her man."

"To find her a man? That's most unusual. But I can't say I blame her."

"No, not *a* man, *her* man. Husband. Has she ever been married?"

She looked at me with sorry eyes. It wasn't clear who she was sorry for. I think she was sorry for a lot of things.

"Mr. Murphy, that wasn't fair to you. I will tell you what I know, though I don't like to discuss another's affairs."

We sit down in her tiny parlor. The only other room is the kitchen, just visible beyond.

"Vera Simms," she says, not like gossip, but halfway between giving testimony and telling a youngster the facts of life, "has never to my knowledge been married. I can't say for sure, she tells so many stories, but it is hard to imagine that she has. For one thing, she lacks the most elementary knowledge of the physical realities of man and woman. I have tried, very gently, to enlighten her, but I think that she doesn't want to know."

I'd basically expected this. But, still, I feel a little sick.

"The most likely thing, of all she's told me, crying on my shoulder from time to time, is that she was indeed engaged, but the man broke it off with her. Died, she would have it, on the way to the altar, but that's tripe."

I growl, "Tripe is right."

She leans back a bit. "I shouldn't have used that expression. I'm sorry now. Vera's fantasies are unfortunate, and I'm sorry she has involved you. But she means no harm, she cannot help herself. I choose to be kind."

Feeling small, I thank her and go out.

Leads, and dead ends, and a probable upshot. But I have to make sure.

I call the number Vera gave me — I'd forgotten it, but it's in the

book. She answers in a dreamy voice.

"Mrs. Bosworth, this is Michael Murphy. I'm working hard on your case. Just one thing that would help us in our investigations. When did you and Roger get married?"

"As I mentioned, we met in April, fifteen years ago today. Love was immediate, marriage came quickly. I was a June bride."

I thanked her and went down to the records office. No records of anyone of either name getting hitched.

But on a hunch, I checked back at the library, their newspaper archive. Sure enough, there was a Roger Bosworth, a lieutenant in the Navy, died valiantly in action sixteen years ago, written up big in the local papers. There was a photograph — good-looking bugger, I had to admit that. Long account, how he did this, that, and the other thing. Mourned by all who knew him, including his fiancée — but it was not Vera Simms.

I go back to the office, feeling sick to the stomach. Joey is there, looking frustrated. He's come up with a pencil from somewhere, and has been covering the table with charts.

"I don't get it, Murph," he says as I come in. "It just doesn't figure. The gin, the note, the disappearance, the stonewalling at the club — it doesn't add up."

"It adds up, Joey. It adds up to zero. The dame's been taking us for a ride. She was never married, probably never met Bosworth, sure as heck never had any estate. She's out to lunch, Joey, she's lunchin' on us, and we been pickin' up the check."

Joey's eyes drop. "Ya know, Murph, acchally, I'm not all that surprised to hear that. It acchally iksplains a few things."

"It explains that we been had. Plus I been to her apartment building, and it's a dump. It's a cinch she can't pay us. She doesn't have a dime to her name."

Joey nods his head sadly.

"And right now I'm goin' over there and tell her where to get off, but good."

Then sadly, but very definitely, Joey shakes his head.

"Look, she may be a dizzy dame, but she's people, Murph. So what if she gets on a high horse. You gonna take her down just fer that? It's what she's gotta do, ta keep her head on. I mean, the things you and I do, Murphy, I mean, let's not throw stones."

Dang it, he's got it again. "Yer right, Joey. Let's break it to her gentle."

"N-no-o, no, Murphy, nothin's gonna get broken, not in this case.

Here's what we do."

I listened, and heck, my hat's off to the brother. We each shave and get a haircut, then head over there together, wearing the best clothes we own.

She opens to us slowly, looking at us with something like fear.

I take off my hat and we walk in.

"Mrs. Bosworth, what I have to say may pain you. But I must ask you to be brave."

She pales, she looks from side to side, she passes her hand over her head.

"When your husband disappeared, he was on a mission, one of the utmost importance to the security of these United States. For six months, he was under deep cover. He was desperate to communicate with you, and it burned in his heart that he could not. But he told himself that just this one time, he would put the freedom of the planet before his private passion — his passion for the woman he loved."

The color has returned to her skin. She is listening with eyes closed.

"Six months went by, risking incredible dangers. At the end of those six, terribly outnumbered, he fell victim to an enemy bullet, in the course of saving the life of a child. With his dying breath, he said your name. And he left — this: for you."

Solemnly, my eyes not wavering, I hold out to her: a red rose.

She gathers it up the way you would a child, sighing so softly I can hardly hear. The thorns prick her, but she does not notice. She breathes deeply, filling her lungs with the scent.

The last rays of the afternoon are straining through the dust-stained windows of her tiny apartment.

"Oh, Mr. Murphy — and you too, Mr. ... Murphy — how can I ever, ever thank you enough? You have returned the water of life to my soul."

I nod, and pick up my hat to go.

She puts her hand to her breast and gives a little laugh through the last of her tears. "Oh! But what am I thinking. I never paid you what you have so richly earned. Here, allow me to write you a check this instant."

I turn, already on the threshold. "That's okay, Mrs. Bosworth. We only charge when we bring 'em back alive."

~ *The End* ~

Tips for Small Businesses

"Y'know, Joey, I'm startin'a think we need to change our sign. That "Discretion Assured" business ain't doin' it. Never was too sure what it meant anyway, looked classy in the magazine we got it from, but I think maybe some people are takin' it the wrong way. We don't do divorce cases, we don't set up hits, and no repo: but it seems like our only would-be clients these days are guys want me to finger his wife to the hit-man and then go repo his ring from her corpse. What're we supposed to do? Do I gotta put up a new sign: "Murphy Bros. — Lost Pets a Specialty"? "M. & J. Murphy, Ltd. Your Overdue Library Books Swiftly and Discreetly Returned"?

Joey flips the page of his comic and shrugs. "Dunno, Murphy; it takes all kinds."

"Yeh well: Maybe *it* does, but *we* don't."

As You Were

The bleach blonde come thru the doorway I'm only halfway finish with the day's first beer. I say hi with the eyebrows over the upraise bottle, but I don't put it down. You don't interrupt a man in these things.

"You one of the Murphys?" she says, glancing back at the sign, "Murphy Bros. — Private Investigators" on the cracked glass door: only now it's backwards.

"I'm Murphy," I say. "What's your beef?"

She looks at me suspicious. "You're a gumshoe, right?"

"Gumshoe, what's with gumshoe? Shamus to you."

She looks away. "I can't afford much."

"Me neither. The beef, the beef."

She looks around the room, not like she's on a tour of the old homes of New England. "Can I sit down?"

"I don't know. Give it a try."

"I mean on a *chair*."

Now *I* look around. That's funny, useta be another one.

"Well, here," I say, getting up heavily, the soul of chivalry. "Have mine." I lumber over and sit down on the crate.

"It's about my husband."

"It usuly is."

Her eyes shoot sparks. "Look, just don't crack wise with me, okay? It's been a long day."

I look over at the wall clock, propped up against the wall. "It's only eleven o'clock."

"Yeh, well it's shapin' up to be a long eleven."

I laugh. "Hey, sorry, ya gotta excuse me, I'm always kinda grumpy till I had the morning's malt. Here, have a beer."

She looks at it doubtfully, then shrugs and takes a sip. She puts it half down; thinks; then takes a long draw, a long one. I don't interrupt.

"So," I say, when we're both feeling better. "Your husband lam it out on ya, huh?"

She looks quizzy at me. "How do you know that?"

"Well," I say, "it figures. He been beatin' up on ya, ya go to your mother, ya go to the cops. He disappear, ya come ta me."

"Well, he beat up on me too," she says grimly. "But I can't prove it. But the desertion, you can testify, that I can prove."

"Hey, now, I don't do divorce cases."

She flushes.

I shrug. "Okay. When ya last seen 'im?"

"Yesterday at breakfast."

That caught me in mid-swallow. I choke.

"Yesterday at *break*fast, that's not much of a desertion."

She looks very dignified. "Perhaps not, but he didn't come in last night, and I just know he won't be back later."

I got this sour look back, I'm shaking my head.

"Oh Mr. Murphy," she says earnestly. "You've got to help me. Do you suppose — do you think he might have been kidnapped?"

"Not hardly. Wouldn't you like."

"Just what do you mean by that crack?"

"L-ook, lady, I find him for you, you gonna keep him?"

"Well, I — what business is that of yours?"

"My business is my business. That's the business I'm in."

"Well, if you say so, yes. Probably. Sure."

"H-ho-kay, I guess that's gotta be good enough. Beggars can't be choosy and I'm skint."

Just then Joey stumbles in from the pool room in back. He's still in his pajamas, which for him means B.V.D.'s

"Hey, Murphy," he mumbles, "whereja put the toaster?"

"Morning, Joey. Try under the moose-head, maybe."

"Moose-head's on the crapper. Better not be under there."

"On the crapper? What's it doin' on the crapper?"

"I dunno, Murphy. You do weird things."

The lady's following this like a tennis match, head from one to the other, ka-bong, ka-bong.

"This is ahh, my associate, Mr. Joseph Murphy. He was ahhh, out late last night on a case."

"Yeh, I'll bet."

It was true, though. A case of beer.

"How y'ikspeck me ta make pop-tarts if we don't got a toaster," Joey grumbles, fishing around in the sink.

"Here, I got matches. Do it the Indian way."

"Matches? An open flame? They'll burn up."

"Okay, hold 'em over a cigarette and roast 'em slow." Joey's cussing, rummaging through the broken-dishes-pile.

"Hey look, Joey, I got a client. K? Ya keep it down?"

"Oh hey, sorry, Murphy, I didden know." His eyes come into focus and he spots her and grins and waves.

"All right, now, name," I say, leaning towards her and getting very businesslike.

"Mine or his?"

"Oh, lady, lady, either one, both. Unlest the one's named Pat and the other Kim I reckon I can figure out who's the john, who's the jane."

"My name is Shar-lene Hunter. My husband's Biff."

"Good. Good classic names. None a this unisex stuff. Okay so, Biff. Where he like ta hang out?"

She curls her lip. "Boko's Pool Hall. They call it a pool hall but they got a bar, too."

"Tch tch tch." I shake my head. "Family man does his drinking at home. Any kids?"

"No kids."

"None in the oven?"

"Mister — No!"

34

"He take the car?!!

"He took his car. I still got mine."

Good, I think. Just so long as you got yours.

She leaves after I get a few more names and places to check out. I got the phone book open and I'm getting out numbers, find out what's open and who's home.

Joey comes in from the landing where he found the toaster and now he's whistling, in a good mood. "Make ya a pop-tart, Murphy?"

"Yeh. We got any blueberry?"

"Blueberry, strawberry, blackberry, raspberry..."

"Beerberry?"

"Oh hey, that'd be good."

Just then another guy comes in from the landing, looking extraught.

"My wife been here?"

"Maybe, maybe, but I ain't been pokin' her, so calm down. Why you think she been here?"

"Because I spotted her car in front of the building, and the other rooms are vacant. Except for the bodega downstairs, that's closed."

"Her car? Hey, what's your wife's name?"

"Shar-lene — but who knows what she told *you*."
He's looking at me with squeezed lips.

"Look I toleja, I ain't been shaggin'er. Shar-lene ... mm ... Hunter?"

"That's right."

"Yeh, she been here."

He glares at me as Joey brings over a plate of pop-tarts. I start to nibble one dainty around the edges, just the little thin crust part. Then — GLOM — the whole fat fruit part, all at once.

"What was she doing here."

"What're *you* doin' here?"

"She ran out on me. I think she's having an affair. She locked me out last night, but I came back this morning just as she was driving away. I followed her, lost her, then spotted the car down a side street, in front a this building. Only I was on a one-way street and I'd just gone past the turn. By the time I got here, she was gone."

"Ye-eh ... Look, say, Biff, why'ncha pull up a chair an' have some breakfast, long's yer here."

"Oh — why, thanks." He sits down on the crate, no complaining. "Yeh I, guess I haven't eaten. — Hey, how d'you know my name?"

"Ya see the sign? I'm a detective. We got our methods. The little dry cells."

He digs into the pop-tarts, piled high like pancakes.

"Y'know, case you're still suspicious, just put two and two together like the gumshoes do. Or in this case, subtract."

He swallows enough to clear his mouth and says, "I don't get it."

"Look. You been following your wife, you lost her, and you seen when she drive away. How much is left over — ten minutes?"

"Something like that."

"Well, that's a mighty quick quickie, drive all that way."

"All right, all right, I guess that lets you out. But why'd she come here?"

I rub my chin. "Don't think I can tell you flat out. Something about shamus/dame privilege."

"Okay, just tell me this. Ya know the address where she was headed? The guy she was gonna see?"

"What's it to ya?"

"Oh, you want your cut, huh. Well it's worth fifty. Cause when I find her I'm gonna blow the both a them away."

"No you're not."

"What're you — Hey, though, you're right. I got a better idea. You're a P.I., right? You come with me, we catch them at it, then you're a witness, and I nail her in court."

"Yeh only, I don't do divorces."

He looks around the office. "I don't see where a cheapskate like you can afford to play so hard to get."

"I can't," I say. "But I do."

Joey's gone out to the gerbil races. Biff is sitting over the breakfast dishes, finishing up with a smoke.

The phone rings. "Murphy speaking ... Yeh, that's right, I ain't been out ... I know that ... Yeh, I'm that too ... What, you want your money back? That's funny, you ain't even paid me. Anyhow, I got a break in the case ...

Sorry, can't reveal my methods. Us armchair guys is got all kina tricks ... Yeh, come on over."

I turn to Biff. "Someone I'd like ya ta meet."

He grins. "A broad?"

"Yeh. "

"Good-lookin' ?"

"Not for me to say. See what you think."

"Yeh," he says, settling back. "I think I might be up for some a that."

My eyes narrow. "You might huh. Minute ago you were ready to blow her away for doin' that."

"Ah, heck. For a man, it's different."

"For a man, it's ig*zackly* the same."

"No no, you don't get the picture. See, I ain't been gettin' it at home."

"So well then, don't take a detective, figure out, she ain't been neither."

"Yeh well, you worry about you, I'll worry about me."

"Fine. Start worryin'. Whacha gonna do if your wife just suddenly walk in here?"

"Ha!" he snorts. "She ain't gonna do that."

Just then, his wife walks in.

"You." She says.

He says: "You."

They're standing, glaring.

Me, ever the perfect host. "Yeh well, now we made our introductions, why'ncha both sit down."

She takes the chair, he takes the crate. Me I sit/lean on the table.

"Where were you last night." She says it, not like a question.

"At Boko's."

"At least you're honest."

"Yeh, at Boko's, and then on the sidewalk. I didn't appreciate that."

She shakes her head irritably. "So what you doin' on the sidewalk? None a my business, I guess."

"Yeh, your business. You locked me out."

"Whadaya mean I lock you out? You didn't come home."

"I come home. A little late, like I said. Two o'clock."

"Two o'clock? You call that a little late?"

"Okay a lot late. But I come."

"Well, I went to bed at twelve."

"So you locked me out."

"Not *out*, I locked *up*. Like always. You want me to be raped in my bed?"

He grinned a little. "Might not be such a bad idea. Dependin' on the guy ..."

She blushed, and then couldn't hold back a little corner of a smile. "Well, if you were ready ... able ... sober ..."

"I'm sober right now," he says.

She lowers her eyes, but then he flares up. "Unless you're sore, from gettin' it elsewhere."

Her mouth pops open but she can't speak. I shake my head.

"A bum rap, Biff. She come here to ask me to find you." Now he blushes, and they both calm down.

"Look, the both of you," I say. "A little advice. From a bachelor and a numbskull, but it's cheap at the price."

They look at me. I don't believe what I'm sayin'. Murphy the marriage counselor.

"Go home, and do what you were talkin' about. And afterwards, go out for pizza — ya listenin'? Get a big one, with everything, largest they got. I don't want you fightin' over the slices."

She sidles over, hooks her arm in his, and his hand kind of walks around her waist. They look at each other, and nod.

"You're okay, pal," he says with a half smile and he gets out his wallet. "What do I owe you?"

"Forget it," I say, already opening the next beer. "I toleja, I don't do divorce cases."

~ *The End* ~

MURPHY ON "LA DIFFÉRENCE"

Like see — if a **man** asks me, How are ya, that's one thing; I don't even think about it. But if a **woman** asks me, How are you, it's completely different; it's even a completely different question, I don't even know how to answer it. "How are you" like, do you mean, How *am* I? is that it? Or is it like: How am — *I, me, Murphy*? Or even: *How* am I, *how, how*, how does it come about? And I'm like — that's a very difficult question, lemme think about it, need maybe a few days to think about it, I'll get back to you, Can I get back to you? You gimme your phone number, I get back to you? I get back to you we, maybe discuss it over dinner? 'Cause it's complicated. Maybe dinner and then, maybe afterwards, maybe we have sex. Good plan? Because, how *are* you, how you *are*, that is very hard to answer, best thing is to have sex first and then think about it, because then at least you aren't distracted and you can focus on the essential thing. — Gosh, you do ask difficult questions. Starting right out with it, too. Whyncha ask me like something about quantum mechanics, I might have better luck with that.

JOEY GOES IT ALONE

On another occasion, owing to an overindulgence, Mr. Murphy found himself temporarily indisposed. Hence it fell to Joseph Murphy, Michael's brother, boon companion and junior member of the firm, to answer the door one rainy noon in September, when a distinguished-looking stranger of medium build rang the bell and, finding this out of order, knocked.

It will immediately be wondered what a distinguished or even a merely sober stranger would be doing repairing to the offices of the brothers Murphy. These — or rather this, for the office consisted of but a single room, besides an incredibly cluttered storage room in back, which principally contained a pool table — were not calculated to beguile the eye. Their listing had lapsed from this year's phone book, though the visitor might have had access to last year's. Or perhaps he had been in the neighborhood, and had noticed the sign at street-level which read, in large letters, "Murphy Bros. — Private Investigators," and then in slightly smaller letters, "Discretion Assured." And then in still smaller letters, "One flight up." Time had not dealt kindly with the calligraphy, which had been restored to near legibility, if not to elegance, with a felt-tip pen. But the only sort of person who just happens to be in this particular neighborhood is the sort normally *pursued* by investigators public and private, not the sort who hires them.

The truth is that the stranger had reasons of his own for selecting the Murphys, rather than some more conspicuously located, reputable, or discerning Private Eye.

"Mr. Murphy?"

"Yeh. Well, sorta. Call me Joey."

"Fine. Joey, then." The stranger seemed to like this quick familiarity. "I've come to consult you about a little problem."

"I get it. Somebody disappeared, and you want me to find them."

This time the stranger was not pleased. His eyes narrowed, and the earlier appearance of joviality now left them instantly. "How did you know that?"

Joey chuckled. "Oh, we got our methods. S'anyhow, what's the dope?"

The stranger waited a moment before replying, but whatever doubts he may have had he set aside for now. "I want you to locate my missing friend."

Joey's ample face broke into a grin; seeing which, the stranger recoiled, and resolved to stop postponing his visit to the dentist.

"Your buddy, huh? Say, that's great. Most people come in here, it's a spouse they wanna find, or a kid. The spouse, they might not even like'm, but they need the support, or they don't wanna get suspicioned of bumpin'em off. And the kids — whoh! — I wonder why the parents even bother. But you, *you* just wanna find yer friend. Yer all right!"

The visitor seemed embarrassed by this accolade. "Yes. Well. I'll be most grateful if you can find him. His name is Richard Malroy."

"Milroy, huh — oh, Malroy? Hey, you gotta pencil? Lemme write some a this stuff down."

The stranger discovered to his irritation that he had only a very good, rather expensive pen. With this he reluctantly parted, and Joey began to apply himself industriously to blocking out the letters of the name, Christian and surname, on the back of a piece of cardboard, the front of which depicted a tiger enjoying a bowl of cereal. By the time he had finished, he had run out of space.

At this juncture the stranger became aware of a moaning issuing from the back room.

"What is this, you got a captive back there?"

"Huh? Oh, that? No, that's Murphy. He's not feelin' too good." The stranger accepted this explanation with indifference, and was about to say something, when the unmistakable sound of billiard balls clicked through the door to the storage room, followed by a loud crash.

"He's sick, and he's shooting pool?"

"Yeh, he likes it, good for the soul." This sentiment was punctured by a muffled groan from the rear.

The stranger shook his head and brushed the air with his hand, as though to say this did not concern him.

"How long's'e been disappeared?" said Joey, taking the course of the investigation firmly in hand.

"Since this morning."

"? — since — ?" Joey gaped, and then leaned back, smiling a would-be reassuring smile. "Oh hey man. No need ta get worked up about it. He probly just went fishing."

"Went — *fishing*?" The stranger scowled. He had deliberately avoided any possible super sleuth, but he didn't much fancy a moron, either. When it came to the support of morons, he gave at the office.

"I hardly think he would have gone fishing."

Joey furrowed his brow. "Well, bowling, then. Does he like bowling?"

"How should I know?"

Joey seemed mystified. "What — you're buddies and you don't go bowling? How can that be?" And at that he became a little less mystified. He said evenly: "Does he like poker?"

"I have no idea."

"Wrestling? The races?"

"Mr. Murphy, it would be more profitable if we — "

"He-ey. Waaaaaait a minute. You say you're his best buddy and you don't even know does he like bowling, or fishing, or ..."

"I did not claim to be his 'best buddy'. I merely said, friend. In an extended sense. An associate, really."

"Oh. A 'sociate, huh. *Extended*, you might say. What kinda 'sociate."

"Well, a business associate."

Joey got canny again. "I ... see ... He skip out on ya, huh?"

The stranger started from his chair. "No — no! What gave you that idea? Ridiculous! We're like this and this!" He locked his fingers in an intimate embrace. Joey looked on with interest. The hands of a strangler.

"Okay, listen. I, ah, gotta consult with my partner."

"Your partner?"

"The guy in back."

The stranger scowled and nodded.

Joey went back to the poolroom, knocked lightly, and opened.

"There's a guy here, Mike ..." The rest of the conversation was lost as the door closed softly behind him. In a few moments, Joey emerged.

"He says o.k., but you gotta pay us."

"Pay you? Don't you usually charge for your services?"

"Oh we do, we do, we just usuly don't collect. But see Murphy's sick, and the teevee's in hock, and we wanna get it out so's he kin just lie ona pool table and watch wit' one eye. He's feelin' a little shaky to be shooting pool — " another crash added weight to this diagnosis — "an'it's just a lot easier. So it'll be fifty up front in your case."

"F-fifty up front." The stranger kept a straight face. "And — in back?"

"Well ya don't hafta pay it in back, cause you fork it up front, see? Cash. Str-r-r-rictly cash. We only take good, clean cash." And, truth to tell, usually not even that.

The stranger nodded and extracted a fifty from among several in his billfold. He had come to the right place.

Joey examined the front and back of the bill, and bit it experimentally, like they do on TV; then, satisfied, went over and deposited it in a cookie jar in the shape of a well-fed bear. Then he came back, and his face fell. "Hey wait a minute, I just remember something. I don't think I can take your case."

Again the narrow eyes. "And just why not?"

"Well see, Mikey, that's my brother, he's my partner, right now not feelin' too good, he mostly does the legwork and the brainwork. Me I'm along for muscle and moral support. So you say I gotta find a guy, where do I look, next door? I got no idear."

The stranger smiled and relaxed. "That won't be a problem. I simply take you to the restaurant I've traced him to — "

"Hey wait a minute, wait a minute. You already know where he is and you want me to find him? Whadaya need me for?"

"Oh well there now, you are still very much needed. It's a very *large* restaurant, and he could be anywhere. He could be in the Oak Room, the Grill Room, or even upstairs in the Blue Room. All of them with both smoking and non-smoking sections. He might even have stepped out to the cloak room. He could even be in the bar."

"Hm. Could be hard ta find him, huh?"

"Yes. All you will have to go on is this photograph," and he extended a black-and-white snapshot.

"Hm, I reckon I could handle that. Hey only, wait a minute. How come you can't do it?"

"Ahh, because I want it to be a surprise. I will be elsewhere, making preparations. When you find him, I want you to bring him to my cabin. When he gets there, he gets a surprise."

Joey's not sure he likes it. "What kina cabin?"

"Why, it's a — it's a *fishing* cabin! You see, I was only joking when I said he didn't like fishing. He loves it. He lives for it. And I am going to offer him some of the ve-ry fi-nest fishing ..." The stranger ground his teeth.

Joey's still skeptical. Comes with his training. "Yeh well, how come a surprise."

The stranger looks up startled. "Why, why, it's his *birthday*!"

"O-o-oh ... Yeh okay, that iksplains it. So what, I bring him to the cabin, an' en ..."

"And then you drop him off at the foot of the path that leads from the road to the cabin, and you don't get out of the car, and you drive away very quickly, and you forget all about it and go spend the fifty however you please. Treat yourself to a pizza, with all the trimmings. You deserve it."

"Sounds good. Only — he-ey-y, how do I know I'm not kidnapping him or somethin'? How do I know you're really his friend?"

"Very good. Oh, very good." The stranger's face is animated with appreciation. "I like to see a man who considers all the possibilities. Your brother underestimates you; and, if I may say so, you underestimate yourself."

"Yeh right, well, so okay, so how do I know."

"Be-*cause*," said the stranger, leaning forward intimately, "because all you have to do when you see him is say, 'Mr. Carnoso sent me. Come with me.' See? He comes voluntarily, of his own free will. You won't even need a gun."

Joey turns it over in his mind. "Hm, sounds on the up 'n' up. Okay, how do I find the cabin?"

"I've written out directions. And we'll first swing by the road that leads there from out of town, so you'll recognize it later, and head from there to the restaurant, just to make sure there's no slip-ups or delays. All you have to do from the restaurant is retrace your steps. And for the further portion, I've traced out the route on a map."

He produced a wilderness map printed largely in light green ink, with a route traced out in red.

Joey studied it. "Fishing, huh."

"Yes, fishing."

"There's no lake."

The stranger frowned and looked at the map. "Brooks. There's brooks."

"I don't see any brooks."

"It's these wiggly lines here. All over everywhere. The place is lousy with brooks."

"I see. With fish in'em."

"Yes. Trout. Mackerel. Salmon. *Swordfish*. You name it. Just busting right out of the brooks."

"Hm, okay. I guess it's on the level. When do we start."

The stranger's face set hard. "Now."

The rain had let up a little. There was some hope of an early return to autumn crispness.

The stranger drove a budget model rent-a-car, and Joey followed on behind in the old Pontiac. They stopped at the turn-off out of town, then doubled over to the belt-road and drove at a moderate speed to the restaurant, the stranger thoughtfully stopping at yellows and checking his rearview mirror to make sure he hadn't lost his tail.

The restaurant was a sort of roadside mansion in an early style, which announced itself as the Carlton. A smaller sign said "Country Inn." That was all there was. No "Good Eats" or "Cold Beer" or "Fine Food and Drink." You just had to know it, or figure it out.

"Good luck," said the stranger through a crack where the window was rolled down just a bit, then sped off in a cloud of dust.

Joey walked through the door and was met by a small dapper man whose professional appearance of graciousness faded a bit when he saw Joey. "Would you care for a necktie, sir?" he said, bowing slightly and offering one from a box.

"Nah, never touch the stuff. Look pretty funny on a t-shirt, anyway," said Joey, and pushed past.

The man ran around and stopped again in front of him. "Have you a reservation, sir?"

Joey looked down at him. "Yeh, me I got *lotsa* reservations, but don't bug me and maybe I won't act on'em. Ya seen this guy?" He held out the photograph.

The man stared at Joey, then glanced quickly at the photograph and back.

"I see. You are with the police? Plainclothes?"

"Very plain clothes. Ya seen 'im?"

The little man cricked his neck at it, though the photo was only a few inches from his face, pursed his lips, and nodded. "One of our steady customers. He may well have come in today."

"So where do I find him."

"I believe he favors the Oak Room. You're not staying for lunch, are you? Then it's all right. Just find your man and, help yourself to a dinner mint on the way out." And with that, the man walked off.

As a trained detective, it did not take Joey long to spot the large varnished wooden sign, oak for all he knew, that read "Oak Room" in rustic letters. He stepped in and looked around suspiciously.

The stranger had been right, it was a large restaurant. This room alone was larger than an entire Burger Queen. And the non-smoking section in itself was hard to find; the whole room was bathed in a bluish haze.

Joey scanned the room without finding anyone familiar. Well, this was where he earned his pay.

He went around from table to table, leaning forward, scrutinizing each face, restraining himself from sampling some of the extra food. He realized it was late lunch-time and he hadn't had a bite all day. Most of the diners seemed not to welcome his inspection: conversations stopped, cigars froze in mid-air. Joey was not enjoying this. He is sensitive and does not take kindly to unkind looks. He thinks: Hey, there gotta be a better way.

He finds it. "Hey, Richard Marlowe!" he bellows in his impressive baritone. Some diners look up but no-one says anything. Then Joey frowns and extracts a large folded-over cardboard from his pocket. "Make that Malroy." Looking up, and louder. "Richard Malroy! Message for Mister Malroy!"

A voice answers from the back of the room, "Over here." Joey goes to where a beckoning finger is protruding up over the smoke.

It is a small, two-person booth, with only one person. "Richard Malroy?"

"That's me. Who are you?"

Joey breaks into a grin. "Joey Murphy. Please ta meecha," and he extends a hamburger hand.

Malroy takes it. Joey shakes heartily, then sits down with a whoosh. "Boy, you sure save me some trouble. I wooden really reconnize you from your photograph," he says, and extends the likeness, now quite crumpled, for Mr. Malroy to inspect.

"Not a very good profile, I'll admit. Say, who took this? Where did you get it?"

"From your friend, paid me fifty to find you. Can you figure that? Fifty big ones, just to find you like this."

Malroy is looking hard at Joey, not unfriendly, just sizing him up.

He licks his lips from the inside, just the very tip of the tongue. "Which friend would that be?"

Joey shrugs. "Mr. Carnoso. I think that's the name he gave. One a them wop names. Or spic names. I don't know. — Hey no offense, right? You're not a spic, right? Malroy? See I don't speak spic. And no offense now, I'm worse than that. Me, I'm a mick." He laughed good-naturedly. "Spics and micks — same deal, some ways."

"No, no offense. My friend, eh?"

"Well, your business associate. Your fishing buddy. Hey, you mind if I join you? Gosh that smells good. I ain't ate all day."

Malroy gives a broad smile. "Sure, be my guest. It's on me."

"On you? Oh hey, that's white a ya! But hey, lemme it least get the beers." He turns around at the waist and waves energetically at one of the waitresses. She pauses, purses her lips, and then comes over. "Hiya honey, big pitcher a pils, willya? And keep'em comin'." She nods and goes off.

"Carnoso, huh," says Malroy when she is out of earshot. "You got the name right, okay. He wants to see me?"

"Yeh, I'm supposed ta take ya to him, up at the fishing lodge. Only first let's have lunch."

"Hm. And how come he couldn't come himself?"

"Well see, he's putting up the decorations, count a it's your birth— Oh, gosh, I gone in done it. Now it won't be a suprise."

"Oh hey, don't take it so hard. I won't tell him you told."

"Aw gee, thanks. Hey, whadda you recommen' ona menu? Lotta strange stuff."

"Well, the rillettes are good, for starters. — No, forget it, I get the picture. Why don't you just order the chateaubriand. That's beef."

"Shat-oh — Whew, more spic talk! *You* tell her, okay? — Mm, hey, good beer. Hey, I never had this. What's it called?"

"I believe it's from Bohemia. Urquell, I believe, or something quite similar."

"Bohemia! Wow, they got spic *beer*, too! Not bad, though, I gotta hand it to'em. Lotta flavor — it's like beer concentrate."

Malroy smiled. "You know, Murphy, you're all right."

Joey smiled back. "Call me Joey."

Three hours later, the Oak Room had pretty much cleared out, especially around their booth. Six pitchers were lined up like soldiers along the edge of the table, three in each rank. The table and the surrounding floor looked like a field after a particularly productive battle. The whole area was richly littered with little pretzel bags, for which the management had had to send out.

The maitre d' appeared in person with the check. The waitress had long since given up. "Are you ... quite done, sir?"

"Sure, sure, all finish'. Gimmeda bill. An' don' worry abouta damage."

"We won't, sir. It's on the bill."

"Shwell. Lessee, oh yeh ..." He studied it hazily, and Joey craned his head around.

"Hey, Rickey, what're those numbers?"

"Wha — those there? Atsa price-a-da meal. An'ats, 'ats forda chandelier."

"That's just forda *meal*? What is this, like, in pesos?"

"No, hey, don' worry aboudit. It's my tab."

"Oh yeh but, remember but, I was gonna pay forda beer. How much that come to?"

"How much you got?"

"Oh hey, lessee, about, about fi' dolla'. Plus a coupon. Ya think they'll take a Burger Queen?"

Malroy threw back his head and laughed. "You're all right, Joey! Forget aboudit, isson me. C'mon, less' breeze."

They broze, Malroy leaving a mound of bills on the plate behind them.

"Jeesh," Joey muttered as they reached the parking lot. "Me I'm oweez findin' things. Now I gotta find my car."

They stood a bit, Joey scratching his head and blinking at the late afternoon sunlight, now bursting forth from behind the clouds. "Is gotta be around here somewheres ..."

"Hey look, there it is," said Malroy, pointing.

"What? Hey, yer right. Only ... Howju know?"

"W-e-ll ..." Malroy splayed his hands and spread his fingers. "It looks, Joey, looks a little differnt from some o' the other cars in the lot."

Joey looked around vaguely, then shrugged.

"Awright, climb in." It wasn't locked.

Joey backed out fast and came to an abrupt stop. "Ooh, musta smunched inta that telephone pole. You think we maybe oughta get coffee?"

"Naw, the breeze'll sober us up."

"Yeh right, the roof, I know what you mean. Sort of a convertible hardtop, what you can't convert it back. — Ooh, hey, lookit. We loss tracka the time. Okay, let's roll."

"So where're we heading?" said Malroy when the road had cleared their heads.

"To the cabin."

"To the cabin?"

"Yeh, remember, the hunting lodge. No, fishing. Whatever."

"Bowling. Maybe it's a bowling lodge."

"Yeh! Heh! I knowju like bowling," said Joey, turning towards his new friend. "Carnoso had it all wrong."

"Wow! Hey, just watch the driving. — Carnoso, eh?"

"Yeh, the guy what sent me. He's waitin' for ya up at the lodge."

Malroy stroked his chin. "Carnoso. What's that fat slob doin' outa the city? I didn't think he ever left his den."

"Oh well hey, he's not that fat. I mean listen, you got present company. If that guy's fat, then I'm — "

Malroy looked over sharply. "Not fat, huh. Maybe it's just because he's so short that it looks that way on him."

"Oh, well, short?" Here Joey looked doubtful. "I mean he's maybe little shorter'n me, but I wouldn't say *short*, not *short* short. Bout the same size as Murphy — my brother Mike."

"Hm. Say, where is this cabin exactly?"

"What, you never been there? Oh, you'll love it. Great place. Sounds like."

"Um. Where."

Joey nodded towards the glove compartment. "There's a map in there … Yeh that's right, next ta the cans."

Malroy studied it with interest.

"It's way out there."

"Yeh, you know, the rural retreat. Hunting, fishing, bowling, you name it."

Malroy nodded, quite sober now. "Somebody's fishing, and somebody's hunting, all right."

They drove on for a while in silence, then Joey said, "Ya mind if I sing? On long trips, I like ta sing."

"Go ahead — that's fine — be my guest."

Joey's great lungs filled with air, and the trees — for they had turned off into the woods on a gravel road — reverberated with song. "Hundred bottles a beer ona wall, hundred bottles a be-e-e-e-er …"

They came at last (at thirty bottles) to the access road indicated on the map.

When they were within a few hundred yards of the expected location of the cabin, Malroy said to stop the car. "Let's surprise him," he said, "and walk up."

"Yeh, great idea!" said Joey. "He was gonna suprise you, and I messed it up, so let's us suprise *him*!"

"That's the spirit. Quietly, now."

They crept up a hillside of clover and tall grass. The sun was now in full possession, and the birds, invisibly high in the trees, celebrated its return.

Halfway up the hill they could see the cabin. They still hadn't come to any streams.

"Gosh, it's smaller'n I thought ..." Joey wondered, becoming a bit disconcerted.

"Shh. Not a sound now. You go first."

Joey happily took the lead. He couldn't recall when he'd had such fun. The drive, the hike, the fresh clean air, all was reviving his senses. By now, there was even a view. When he came to the faded wooden porch and clunked up it, he could not restrain himself from once again bursting into song.

"Happy Birth Day To You-ou-ou ... ," he bellowed as he burst marching through the door.

He had heard the clunk and dived for the dresser, but he was the victim of a triple element of surprise. First, he had given up on them. Probably that imbecile couldn't find the place, or he'd been double-crossed.

Second, the door had been locked, which should have given him time, but the jamb splintered — a cheap door. Third, when he looked up, hand still in the top drawer, he didn't see Malroy. Just the lamebrain walking side of beef. He froze.

Observing him through the window in that position, Malroy entered, casually holding a gun.

"So it's you, Ferret. I though it might be."

Joey looked from the one to the other, confused. "Ferret? What, Ferret Carnoso?"

"No, Jim Ferret. As in rat."

"You're the rat, Malroy, selling us out to Carnoso like that! You figured you'd be long gone by tomorrow, take the money and run! Well I got news for you, buddy, I come back early, and I tumbled to your little game. Yeh, Rosie, it was Rosie that tipped me. You thought you had her in the palm of your hand!"

"Hey, wait a minute," said Joey, stepping between them and facing Ferret. "You can't call my buddy a rat."

The move was generously meant, but fatally ill-timed. For Ferret, now suddenly out of the line of fire, rapidly withdrew his hand from the drawer. In it, a .44. It neatly outclassed Malroy's easily concealable but relatively ineffective rimfire .22.

"Outa my way, ox ..."

Now, there were some things Joey minded, and others he did not. Guns left him indifferent. But he did not like being called an ox. With a single movement he swept Ferret off his feet and held him upside-down for inspection, so he could get a good view.

"What'd you say?"

Ferret frankly had not expected interference from this quarter, a man supposedly on his own payroll. He smarted at his miscalculation, and at the sudden reversal of his fortunes in every sense.

"Put me down, you idiot!"

Again, an unfortunate choice of words.

"He-ey, you doan call me dat! Y'know d'lass person call me dat? My firs' gra' teacher. Doan call me dat."

Ferret mustered as much dignity as he could in his position.

"I'm sorry I spoke rashly. No doubt your scores have improved since that time. Now if you'll just — "

"No no, 'at did it for me. After that I give the rest a the grades the miss."

"Fine, fine, I didn't ask to see your report card. Just — " He tried frantically to twist around as he saw Malroy's figure emerging around the side, lowering — no, raising — the gun. "Listen to me, you've got a swindler right behind you, a con man, a sell-out artist, and he's about to add cold-blooded killer to his list."

"Aww, Rickey woulden ..."

"Look, I tell you, he's got a gun!"

Joey hadn't noticed it, so casually cradled in his companion's palm.

He dropped Ferret and turned around. Ferret crashed to the floor and lay crumpled. Malroy managed a smile.

"He's lying, Joey buddy. The man's a snake. You saw how he lied about Carnoso, right? You saw how he lied about the cabin — not a fish for miles around."

"I was wondrin' about that myself. But what's with the gun? You know I don't think those things are even legal, y'know that? Those little Saturday Night jobs."

As he had done before, Malroy licked his lips; but the tongue came out a little further this time. "Yeh, I think you're right. I'll — I'll look into it. Now for just now, just step aside — please — and let me finish this guy."

"What, you crazy? He's not gonna hurcha."

"You saw him, he was gonna blow both of us away!"

"Well, maybe, but he don't look too conscious now." Joey surveyed the heap and shook his head.

"Yeh, but when he wakes up, he'll plug us, and if we're gone, he'll come gunning for us ..."

"Oh, izzat what's gotcha worried. Here, no problem."

Joey lifted the revolver and swung out the cylinder, then smashed it down with tremendous force against the stove, disabling the yoke. Malroy winced.

"Happy?"

"Yeh, uh, thanks. Thanks, that's just great. Only ..."

He had to risk it. The man was big, but not fast. A shot to the leg, a sprint, he could be out to the car. — But the keys, the keys to the ignition!

Well, it would have to be two shots, then.

Would there be time for it? Malroy glanced at Ferret, still unmoving. He looked back at Joey, who was returning the gaze in a strange way. Something like distrust seemed to show in his eyes.

Sweat oozed from Ricky Malroy's forehead, palms, and upper lip. Again the quick lick. Joey seemed to move forward. — Malroy panicked, shot wildly, hitting Ferret in the leg. Ferret gasped and groaned.

Joey's hand swooped down and out, sending the small semi-automatic sailing through a window-pane. Malroy broke into a rage.

"You idiot! Now you've done it."

Joey scrunched up his face. "I don't get it. Everybody calling me a ijjit. What'd I do? Will somebody tell me? Just what'd I do?"

Malroy was fast grabbing back possession of himself. "All right, forget it. I'm sorry, forget it. Just drive me back to town. Just drive, you can drop me anywhere, we'll pass the sponge over, just call it a day."

Joey slowly, slowly shook his head.

Again the tongue, and again the sweat. "C'mon, c'mon, what's the matter. Look, I'll double what he was payin' ya."

Again the shake. "That's not enough, Rickey."

Malroy sneered. "Oh, you want your slice, do you. I mighta known it when you mooched a meal off me."

Joey flinched.

"All right, if it'll buy a drive and your silence, I'll cut you in on the take."

Joey shook his head. "That's not what I mean. Enough reasons. Not cash."

"Heh-he-ey, what is it with you? I make a handsome offer. Where's the problem?"

"You're not my friend."

Malroy laughed, edging towards hysteria. "Oh that's rich! Oh I like that! Oh, break my heart!"

Joey's brow clouded, threatening thunder and rain. "You know I'll tell you who's the ijjit. Cause there's nothing more important than friendship. You make fun a that, you got nothing."

"Yeh — yeh right, sure, take it easy."

"I was *friends* witchoo, er it least buddies, a little bit. Ya don't rat on a buddy."

"Right! So don't rat on me!"

"But I'm figurin' it out. You was never my buddy. Not even it the beginning. You was just in it fer you."

Malroy's grinding his brow with the heel of his palm. "I don't believe it, I got a crazy man. You can't talk reason, you can't talk money. The man's a crazy man."

Joey puffed in disgust. "Ah, the heck wit'it. Gotta go. But you're stayin'."

He looked around the room and found a lamp and a plug-in alarm clock. From these he ripped out the cords. He sat Malroy down very hard on a slat-back chair, hooked his arms back over the top and tied each wrist to the opposite upright. Then he removed Malroy's belt and his own belt, and secured each ankle to a chair-leg.

He set the chair facing the camp bed, where he propped Ferret up, bound his ankles with Ferret's belt, and tied his hands behind his back with a ripped-up bed sheet. Then he splashed him awake with some rusty water from the sink.

"I'll be leaving you two lovebirds. You guys deserve each other. Bet you got a lot to say."

He walked back to his car and drove home slowly in the gathering dusk. This time he did not sing.

When he got home, his brother was already up, and had managed to drag himself to the kitchen table. He waved weakly when Joey walked in.

"How ya feelin', Murphy?"

"Oooh, not so good. But better. How'd your day go?"

"Okay. Here, I broughcha a pizza. Look, anchovies!"

"He-hey-y, good brother," said Murphy, breaking into a brave if dented smile. "You rilly know how ta take care of a guy."

"An' look. Here. I broughcha some beer."

"Tail a the dog! An' oh, he-ey, the cheap kind, the more-for-less. My faverit brand." He popped the tab off a couple and drained them.

"Ah, that's good. — Say, I guess I rilly tied one on last night, huh."

"Ah, heck, it wasn't nothing."

"Did I, did I do anything, you know, weird?"

"Naah, nothin' special, don't worry about it, Mikey. Eat your pizza."

"Ay-men ta that."

He set in munching, and after a while asked, between sips and swallows, "So how'd it go? We got a satisfied customer?"

"No, I don't think so, Murph."

"Coulden handle it, huh, Joey, all on your ownsome? Ahh, don't worry about it. I'll be back in action. Hey, what would you do wit'out me."

"I don't know, Murphy," said Joey simply. "You're my best friend."

~ *The End* ~

Murphy and his Friends

"You seen Charlie?"

"Yeh," says Joey. "He was here earlier. He says hi."

Good, good; I miss Charlie sometimes.

"And oh — hey! Here he comes again! Welcome, little guy!"

We both break into grins. Now ... here he comes, now now ... Charlie the Cockroach. Good ol' little ol' Charlie.

I break off a crumb of my pizza crust, and he goes for it, like always. Never complains, never asks for the pepperoni, or says How about lasagna next time: he just accepts what is given, and is thankful, I guess.

Don't you call me sentimental. I'm not saying Charlie's cute, like a hamster or whatever. Charlie is something that only a mother bug could love — that, or someone who loves just absolutely everything. But hey — he does what he gotta do, to live, to eat, to get around, on his eight legs or ten legs or however much he has. And I get that. And it doesn't cost me nothing, keep him in carbs; that crumb woulda just gone to waste. But like, this way, it's almost like a sort of tiny unfathomable little pint-sized like, cockroach communion ...

And the funny thing is, one time, I found myself, now this sounds weird, but I found myself kind of actually kind of saying almost like a prayer ... for Charlie. Don't get me wrong — just a little small miniature kind of a mini-prayer, it'd fit in a thimble. Went something like — well really I don't even remember it, it wasn't like it was even me saying it, but someone else saying it in me — went something like:

"Yeh. Charlie. Yeh. (Amen.)"

Suddenly Joey says: "Hey, look! Murphy! *Two* Charlies!"

And, dang, the brother's right. Charlie got him a twin!

"C'mon guys," I say. "Plenty 'nuff for both of yas. C'mon, little guys ..."

REVERSE ENGLISH

So anyhow this one time, me and Joey are in the back room shooting pool. Loser to take out the garbage — a lot is riding on this game.

I just pulled off such a sweet shot like you would not believe. Lady Luck's on my side — she been bribed.

I'm calling my shots, you go here you go there, the balls are like these performing fleas — hop! ina pocket, just like I said. Joey's just standing there, stone cold sober. Poor sucker — his whole life must be passing before his eyes.

"Think of it, Joey. Two whole weeks a that goo-o-ood garbage, just waitin' onya, sittin' aroun' in'ese busted twisted plastic baggies and wet rotted-out paper bags and ripped-up pizza boxes with they got this sort of smeared-on paste, oh look my my, what's that falling out ona floor, all overa floor, turns out there was still some crusts in it, those are so-ome happy ants." Pock! "And think a that lo-o-ong narrow staircase down to the dumpster, the one with the burned-out bulb that neither *you's* gonna change it neither *me's* gonna change it, still littered with roller skates and banana peels and ball bearings from last time. — Quiet, Joey, I'm linin' up -my death shot." I lean over, leaning mean, and sight along the cue.

And then: Something isn't quiet.

Joey squints a little and perks up an ear. "You hear something, Murphy?"

"Nothing, Joey." Grimacing.

Joey listens real careful — hard to hear, the pool-room door is closed. "Kind of like — somebody *knocking*, Murphy?"

"Nobody knocking, Joey." I wave it away like a cloud of gnats. "You ain't gettin' out of this *that* easy, Joey." But like a cloud of gnats, it comes back.

"There it is again, Murphy." Joey is listening with increasing interest.

Sweat starts charging out of its dugouts and foxholes and is mixing it up on my brow. "Jeez, Louise, Joey — I'm ona streak! It's just the pipes, there, Joey. Just the plumbing going. Don't break my *streak*!"

But it's back. The knock, the knock from Porlock.

Joey's got his head tilted thoughtfully to one side. "Pipes don't knock 'Shave an'a Haircut', Murphy. I'll go see who it is."

So I gotta wait while he's gone. I mean, he *trusts* me, but with stakes this high, a man would be a fool.

Joey comes back in and closes the door. "Customer, Murphy. I told 'im to wait. Let's hustle up and finish this game."

"Good a ya, Joey," I say, gritting my teeth. And I lean for the shot.

But it's no use. Luck — that tramp — has decamped, the magic moment is in smithereens.

P-pock! Oh ... no. Eight-ball, down the hatch.

Joey nods like a wise man. "Don't take it too hard, Murphy. Exercise'll be good for ya. Now let's check out this john."

He's waiting on the one chair, sitting with his knees out and a rolled umbrella chonked down between them. Dark double-breasted suit, deep-purple handkerchief like it's never had to deal with actual snot, peeking demurely out of a breast pocket. A tie like he's mourning for two uncles and an aunt. His cufflinks could be my life savings, if I had any. Black hair neatly combed, and somehow looking exposed — it looks like it'd be happier under the homburg he has set to one side.

"I'm a busy man, Mr. Murphy."

Hey, here's a johnny likes to chew the fat — two seconds and already he's into his autobiography.

"Me too," I say, already not liking the guy. "Just busy with different things."

A little grimace from one small corner of his mouth. "Your associate here told me that you two were in conference. But it sounded as though you were playing pool back there."

"The science of detection," I say, making one of them pointy steeple things with my fingers, "is in many respects like the art of pool." I look around for a pipe but no such luck, and a Camel wouldn't be the same thing, so I open a beer. "The game in question presented certain features of interest."

He stares at me; then scowls and brushes an imaginary cobweb aside. "That's neither here nor there. I've got a job for you."

My eyes get hard. "Spill."

Soon as Joey sees I'm gonna talk to the guy and not give him the brush-off, spite a what he done, he lumbers back off to the pool-room and closes the door. I handle the business end of things.

"I need a man," he intones, "of absolute discretion"; and he hands me his business card.

I toss it aside. "You got one, bub," I reply. "Cancha read?" And I point to the lettering on the frosted top of the door, which, even though it's now backwards, so it's kind of hard to make out, if it was frontwards, then just filling in a letter here a letter there gives you: "Murphy Bros. — Private Investigators — Discretion Assured." Hate it when some folks don't do their homework.

The guy frowns again. Mr. Frownie. Just no pleasing some folks.

"It's my wife," he says. And I think: Uh-oh.

"She's been seeing some people. Stepping out on me. Might be two-timing. Running with a crowd."

Oh no, it's coming.

"I want you to shadow her — find out what their relationship — find out what their *game* is."

I sigh, I shake my head, as the paycheck that now can never be, flutters out the window on little wings.

"I'm real sorry there, Mr. — Mr. — well it doesn't matter now anyway. That just isn't my line. No hits, no repo, and no divorce."

"But — !"

"No-o, don't reach for your wallet." I feel weary, been through it all before. "I know you got enough in there make me drool down my shirt-front, drool into my boots. But I — just — don't — do that kind of thing."

A sad silence lies between us, like a dead pet.

At length he speaks, his cheeks one shade darker. "If you only knew what — well. I won't argue with your scruples, such as they are. My bad luck." He gets up to go.

Inside my head I'm thinking — and inside my empty stomach is rumbling: *Shut up, scruples!* But they won't shut up. Jeezes, sometimes I'd like to strangle those guys.

He rises — simply, sadly. "Good-bye, Mr. Murphy."

"Yeh, g-bye," I mumble, miserable, not getting up. He goes to the door and walks out of my life.

Time does its number, second hand skipping, the big hand budging, the fat hand like it's on downers; but me, I haven't moved. And when I hear a heavy step outside the door, I think: Oh; and then think nothing. And there's no knock, and the knob turns, and the door swings open, and the frame is crammed full of this — focus, now — interesting guy. His head just brushes the lintel, his shirt barely covers his arms. His face is wide, and it's got this very unique scar. It's like a country road, jagged and meandering. It starts from up over his eye, takes a chunk out of the brow and angles down, hops over the eyes on an imaginary bridge then it's back in business on the nose, up over the hump, down the other side, down; then it crosses the cruel lips, and peters out at the side of the black stubble chin. He shoots the cuffs beneath his dark double-breasted, a touch dusty from going up and down in the earth. I'm following all this with interest; then his eyes get thin.

"You Murphy?"

"You Bozo?"

"I know who's been here."

"Ve-ry good."

He takes a sharp step forward, then checks it. "I got just one thing to say to you."

"Aw, make it two."

His hands ball fists, like it's a spasm, then slowly let go, like escaping steam. "Just one thing, wise guy." He reaches into the side pocket of his striped silk suit, and pulls out a fat roll of twenties, flaps them against his hand. "Yours for the asking. Just *lay off this case.*"

My ears are buzzing. I don't freaking believe this. I've been waiting my whole life to hear that line. This is where I jab his chest with a stubby forefinger and say — heck, I got the whole speech memorized.

Only problem is, I already turned the case down. So what's to stop me taking up the offer? It's free cash.

Then I think of what Joey would say. You can come up with the most brilliant arguments, lay reasons end to end till they circle the globe, it all goes right by him. He'll just say: "Nope. No go."

I hang my head and mumble. "Sorry I ... don't take payments ... ta lay off cases ... " I'm just not up to making the big speech.

He smiles, not a nice smile; you got a smile like that you oughta keep it locked up. "Sorry to hear that, pal, cause that was just the carrot. There's also a stick." And he tugs at a black leather glove that he's wearing on his left — just one glove, studded with metal — pulling it tight over huge knuckles.

Just then Joey comes in from the back room, holding a pool cue. He has to turn sideways to get through the door.

"How's tricks, Murphy? We got a client?"

"Who — Short Stuff here? Naw, he was just leaving. Walk softly, pal."

He backs out, wearing his grit-eating grin. "You ain't heard the last of me, mug."

"Who's the heavy?" says Joey when our friend has left.

"Oh, just some bozo from Gozo, tells me to lay off a case," I remark offhandedly, hiding a touch of pride.

"And you told him where to get off — right?" He looks at me hard.

"Yeh well ... basically. Sorta."

"What's this *sorta*."

"Fact is I, ya see I, I never take the case in the first place."

He looks pained. "Ohh, Murphy, first customer we get in like how long, like a month; and you turn him down? You know the tee-vee's in hock, and the radio — even the *toaster's* in hock, what don't even work, and you turn him down? So hey — what kinda case was it, would it of been?"

I shrug and sigh. "Same old same old. Guy wants me to shadow his wife. You *know* we don't do divorce cases."

And Joey — I never seen him like this — his eyeballs do a little spin in his head, like calculators, like cash registers.

"Course not," he says, a little hoarse, "but I mean, how do you know the dame is really his *wife*?"

"Huh? How you figure?"

He leans forward. "Murphy, Murphy, doncha see it? Palookas like that last guy don't show up outa nowhere and put the muscle on a dick in some dumb-ass divorce case, let alone fork up cash. And how come he'd know what the score was, and who been here, he was just workin' for some ditched dame? No, hey," and here he laid his index alongside his nose, "to me, that guy spells Mob." He nodded significantly. "Emma, Oh, Bee." He's rubbing his hands. "There's gotta be more to it than meets the private eye."

I scratched my head. The brother's got a point there. Maybe. "So, how do you figure it?"

Joey hunches toward me even further, his eyes lit up. "For my money the first guy's in some deep trouble. The dame's a blackmailer, counting on bilking him big. Ya see? The guy's loaded, but he don't want to pay; he just wants her out of the way. But he don't know exactly what she has on him — probably lots to be had, a guy like that — or who she's working for. Probly wants to shut her trap for her, for good, but he figures, whoa, there's a syndicate behind her, looks like; they'll want their cut; she's just a front; wipin' 'er out, there's no percentage.

"So he comes to us. But he don't want his secrets known, him being blackmailed, and what for. So he makes up this songanddance about she's his wife, blah de blah, oh won't she please come home, yadda yah, maybe been two-timing, *sob*, so you got to shadow her discreet. But really, he doesn't want to tip off the Mob guys. I mean, can you blame him? We gotta help this guy."

I'm rubbing my jaw. Yeh, it figures — I guess. "Still, I don't know ... "

"Look, Murphy, you're in it already. That glove guy is gonna be back. Maybe some time I'm not here. Or back with his boys, or a bomb, or just layin' forya somewhere. Man, before all this is over, you prolly gonna get stomped on, shot at, vamped on — "

"Yeh yeh yeh — "

" — horsewhipped, cold-cocked, strangled, burned with cigarettes — "

" — okay okay — "

" — tied naked to a dentist chair while this sado sicko ex-Nazi — "

" — okay *okay*!"

" — ... an' ... an' you gonna go through all that for what, *nothing*? not even a greeting card? for a case you're not even working? I mean, *Murr*-phy-y ... "

I'm stumbling around on the floor looking for that business card I crunched up. I find it in among the popcorn fragments, floating in a pool of beer.

Larsen, huh. Real estate, huh. (I mutter, grumbling and dialing.) A wait — then this little million-miles-away ring. A neutral: "How can I help you?"

"Larsen? No? okay get him. ... — Larsen? Murphy. That case still open? ... 'kay right ... You got yourself a private eye."

We drove down early the next morning, around ten. Downtown's usually pretty crowded that hour, but Joey spotted a fire hydrant and I pulled right in. I just love those things. Just like they had a sign on 'em, "Reserved for Murphy."

We stepped out and stretched and filled our lungs with the smog. It smelled good. Two city guys, out on a case.

Larsen's office was at the tip top of the Akron building. To reach it you had to get into this like velvet elevator, padded like a gangster's casket, with railings of brass. A special elevator that doesn't even bother with the first fifty floors. Elevator operator, dressed in pale grey, black-braided, like a chauffeur only a coupla cuts above dealing with anything so crude as a car. (Wonder if they even got bathroom attendants in this joint. Weirds me out. I gotta piss, I'll go somewhere else. No, get away from me, don't you hand me no towel.)

He inquired after the numerical designation of our floor, kind of frosty, like, Are you *sure* you gentlemen are in the right lift? Poor-folks' elevator over that way, first fifty floors. But when I told him the number — highest number they got — it seemed to impress him, I mean this one hair in this one eyebrow sort of unfroze and maybe twitched, and he duly pressed the switch. It whooshed up and I felt my stomach sink.

"I think I'm gonna lose my lunch," I muttered to Joey.

"Not in here, Murphy," he warned. "Anyhow, three beers ain't exactly lunch."

We step out and there, right there, is the company door, a glowing mahogany, flanked by a couple of urns with a chunk of the Sahara in 'em to stub out your butts. Joey's about to knock on it but I nix that and we just stride on in. It's a reception room, sort of, like at the doctor's, only no Reader's Digests from years gone by, no toys for kids. At a big desk, bigger than my desk, bigger than my office, actually, sits a woman in a mauve blouse, quietly amused. And *that's* just the receptionist.

"We gotta 'ppointment," I say, coming right to the point.

She finds this charming; a silver laugh. I'll never figure dames. "You must be Mr. Murphy. And — ?"

"Joey, my brother Joey."

"Yes of course. Why don't you two gentlemen have a seat and wait."

I didn't like the way she put it. "Naw, we couldn't do that. — C'mon, Joey, we're wastin' our time, let's blow."

We head for the door and she does a double-take and whispers something into an intercom. Suddenly she's all smiles and waves us on. "Mr. Larsen will be pleased to see you now. Do please go right in."

"Yeh," I say, "we'll do that."

The office takes some getting used to at first. Lights dim, like he's gonna show a movie. Potted plants looming around like bodyguards.

I almost stumble in the deep-pile carpet heading towards his desk; hamster might get lost in there for days. I look left, I look right, checking out the joint. Noticing details that might go right by your average man. The walls have got framed paintings on them, that for my money look like finger-painting, but hey, taste is taste. Him he likes stuff like what mothers of toddlers hang on refrigerators. Me I like power-tool calendars with broads.

"*So*," he says, with a wide smile, smile like that you gotta go through a doorway sideways. "I'm glad you gentlemen changed your mind." He waves a hand vaguely, as though dismissing all memory of our earlier disagreement. He rises, goes to a sideboard. "Gentlemen care for a drink?"

Oh hey, a guy after my own heart, not yet eleven and he's offering us refreshment. "Yeh! You got Mickey's?"

He looks a little puzzled, though the smile remains.

"Mickey's Big Mouth. Comes in a like, like this little green barrel, thing, just right to put your fist around. Nice wide mouth so's you can down it in one pop."

He pauses. "I'm ... afraid not. I gather that is a ... an example of the brewer's art? Some variety of ale, perhaps?"

My eyes seek his ceiling. "Is the Pope Polish? Is Murphy horny? Do tomatoes grow on trees?"

"Y-es, I ... see your point. Scotch do?"

"Pour it."

He does, filling a couple of beer steins, basically. The guy's all right. I hate those little shot jobs, like drinking out of a thimble, makes you lift your pinkie automatic. Then, shifting down to business, he lets his voice get a little more hearty and a little more sober, and one note lower. "The deal is this. The woman in question — I mean, my wife — "

Joey gives me a significant look. "Your — 'wife'," I say.

"That's right," he replies, with just a hint of a wink. "My ... ... 'wife'."

I don't like the set-up. I get up from my chair and start pacing around. "Listen, Larsen. I don't care about your private affairs, but if I'm gonna help you, I gotta know the score. Level with me. She's not your wife, is she."

He seemed to falter. "I — I — You're right, Mr. Murphy." He sank back in his armchair, almost as though relieved. "You're a very perceptive man. But she *was* my wife once, she really was. The divorce was messy ... "

Joey grimaced and I added bitterly. "Divorces usually are."

"Yes, well, this one was extra. And she still has it in for me — up to the handle. Look, maybe she did have a legitimate beef, at one time, just like I had mine, but I fixed her up financially she doesn't have to worry for the rest of her life. High style to which she got accustomed, you know the drill. And yet still she — I mean she's *after* something. But what? The rest of what I got? Or something — *more*?"

Nodding and frowning, nodding and frowning; yeh, this guy is in a jam.

"I mean look — "

Murphy looked.

"I try to toe the line, you know, most ways, most the time, but hey, business is business — y'know that? — and things happen, fallout and spillover, stuff you never intended. Unforeseen consequences; some legal, some maybe not. Is that my fault? So what with *this* and what with *that*, well, it got complicated.

"Plus she's got an associate now, or maybe several; and I don't know what their *game* is. Is he close to her, has he got something on her? Who is behind all this? Is he making her do this — or is *she* using *him*?"

Wheels within wheels, and Murphy's mind is spinning. I mulled over what he had told me as I savored the Scotch. Not bad, really — like a beer that's been in a brawl.

"Making her do ... what exactly."

He glanced over at one of the potted plants like there might be a spy behind it. "I can't tell you everything, boys; don't even understand it all myself. It's deep. There are — wheels within wheels."

Joey let out a whistle. "Wheels wit'in wheels, huh! — Hey wait a minute, that dudden even make sense."

"Look, Larsen," I said, ignoring the interruption, "We're gonna help you, we gotta know the score. Who do you think these guys are, what leads do you have, and what do you want us to do about it."

He swallowed hard. "What you *should* do, if there is anything that you *can* do, is not for me to say. We are dealing here with ... " His voice faltered. " ... with desperate men."

Another low whistle from Joey. This beat comic books all hollow.

"Men who will do anything — *anything*. Men who will stop at *nothing* — nothing at all."

Joey clicked his tongue, his hunch confirmed. Turning towards me, he silently mouthed the words: "*The Mob.*"

"So what have they got on you?" I said, not letting up. You gotta keep the pressure up on a reluctant client, make 'em come clean, don't take I-dunno for an answer. They'll be better off for it.

He ran a finger around his collar. "Listen I ... can't quite go into it. Let's just say they've got on my case. And I want to know what's in it for them. And what it'll take to make them back off."

I nodded. Score one for Joey.

"Look," I said. "This is all very nice. But all very vague. You got a line on where I can find these guys?"

He laughed a bitter laugh. "I got an idea where you can find them and you'd be dead the next minute. What you have to do is to catch them off their own turf. And the best way to do that is when one of them is out on his ownsome, loving up Stella."

"Stella?"

"My ex."

I grimaced but I'd known from the start this case wouldn't be pretty.

"There's a roadhouse," he went on, "on the shore, she used to go to sometimes, back when she was two-timing me. Now that she's tied up with this crowd, I figure she might go back." He gave me an address, a color photo of his ex-wife, and a small advance. "Just for expenses, Mr. Murphy. You'll be rewarded handsomely when this is all behind us — when you have got results."

I grunted okay and Me and Joey moved out, back past the receptionist (with her little amused parting nod) and up towards the elevator. Then I nixed that. We took the stairs.

The road ran down near the water, and on a still night like this, you could practically smell the fish. A thick fog held the smells, and dished them up again with second helpings. Joey drove. My head was half hanging out the window, listlessly looking here and there, as though scanning the landscape for clues.

Joey's mostly the silent type, but tonight he was talking nonstop. "I can't believe it, Murphy; a case, a case at last. You know I guess — guess it was getting to me, starting to start getting to me, you'n'me, day after day. Day after day with no case. You know? Starin' downa sidewalk: no case. In the desert, like — gnome sane? an' no oasis. Youn-me, stuckina desert, no oasis, no case. Just shooting pool, and playing the fool. And hoping, someday, someone, somebody would come through that door."

"Yeah," I said, not paying much attention, and squinting a bit to try to make out shapes in the dark. "I know how it is."

"Cos I mean like: listen. Youn-me. Rilly. Meen-you. It's about *time*, bro' — Noam seine? I mean we been *used*, good brother; *used*; used and abused, and we paid our dues, but I'm all confused ... "

My eyes click off the landscape and swivel around. "Dues ain't something you just pay and go home, Joey. It's not like a bill for dry cleaning. You pay, you keep paying; paying, and paying. It's like taxes, only worse. Taxes you don't gotta pay; you don't pay 'em, they catch you, they put you in jail; big deal. But *dues* ... *dues*, good brother ... they just ... keep comin' back ... like a bad memory ... like somethin' ya done, or didn't do ... I mean I'll like — someday, be on my deathbed, someday, all ready to shuck off this vorpal coil and go meet Saint Pete; and it'll be: No Go, Murphy. One more thing you gotta do."

The touring car crested a hill, and the roadhouse loomed into view. We stowed the wagon, way off the edge of the shoulder, well out of sight. We got out and slapped the dust off our hats, then walked the rest of the way. Music was leaking from the windows of the roadhouse, muffled by the fog.

We walked slowly up the broad warped wooden steps, just as a couple of snockered youths clattered rapidly down them, laughing. "Looks pretty lively," I observed, my mind somewhere else.

The door guy looked us over but didn't stop us; my password was my ugly mug. We pushed in and a new fog met us: dryer, of tobacco smoke; anyhow smoke. The din swelled and now sounded friendlier. People were enjoying themselves, having a good time; unwinding from the stress of the day.

At one end, a single big mirror covered the whole width of the wall, inside a horseshoe-shaped bar, surrounding a bare pine board stage, with room for the bartenders to move, silently, in between. Onstage, a humorous-looking old gal (been around the track; been around the bend) was taking it off, taking It All off, over and over, onandoff, onandoff: trying to take her time about it, stretching out the tempo, vamping for a while: but It All was just a black bra and bikini briefs, and there's only so much fiddling you can do, to delay the inevitable. On the far side of the bar, in a pool of light, lay the craps tables, and a single (silently surrounded — hoping, hoping) round spinning giving taking silently mocking roulette wheel. Joey promptly bellied up and ordered six beers.

A couple of heads turned, and I hissed at him. "Joey Joey — get a grip on. Lower the profile, there , Jo'. We supposed t'be under cover." So he shrugged and changed his order to four beers — "A pair more in six minutes." I ordered the same.

We each drained one right out the bottle, right off the bat, to clear the palate; then another couple to clear the head (you can't truly savor a beer on an empty liver); then, sighing, poured the next one into a glass.

The mirror was nice; a nice touch. I might be (seem to be) staring into space, but really watching what was going on (with my penetrating, private-eye eyes), what little subtleties might be playing out, at the far other end of the room. One a those P.I. tricks; I got a bunch of 'em.

The other half of the hall had small darkened tables away from the stage, for people who had already seen the entertainment take her clothes off fifty-sixty times, and had gotten the basic idea: Two tits! No dick! Amazing! Who woulda guessed???

Abruptly, the stripper stopped, and donned a bathrobe; walking nonchalantly off the stage for a cigarette break, at the other, darker, side of the bar. She hopped onto a stool beside a black guy, who started to chat her up; could of been her agent, could of been her friend. She smoking, saying nothing; him going on and on; an animated conversation, nonetheless. Nobody paid either of them much attention.

The bartenders moved smoothly back and forth along the walkway, like sad-eyed priests, responding to forefingers raised half an inch off the bar, by unaccompanied customers with downcast eyes. Or to the barest veiled hint of a glance, which yet spoke with desperate eloquence: *Hit me again.* Silently refilling glasses and mentally adding a total to some abstract tab.

Lot of regulars here. I caught the eye of a barkeep as he glided by and got another two tall ones and some pretzels along with. Could be a long night, and a guy needs protein.

A blonde walked in on a guy's arm — I caught a glimpse of her in the mirror, framed momentarily in the door. I matched her in my mind with the photograph but no match. The blonde and her escort disappeared into the darkness, and a waiter headed off in their direction. Against the far wall, a tall guy was visible in the glow of the jukebox, leaning over it, taking his time, studying his choices. Choose wisely, friend. You only get so many nickels in this life. Then he walked off and an amplified country-sounding guy started to sing of a love gone wrong, blending in with the general din.

The stripper stretched and climbed back up onto the stage like a farmer getting up at six to milk the cows. She hung her robe on the hook that they had for her, and started to grind to the different, stripper's music. Sort of sputtering at first, like an engine warming up on a cold morning. It was fairly okay music, though pointless and loud, but useful for keeping other, troubling thoughts out of your head. She started getting into it and heads nodded and feet got to tapping and a few couples kind of swayed to it, while other guys, lone guys, stared into their beers and sweet sad old times lived again in separate heads. She actually got so into it, more than you'd think, listening it seemed to some other music, at another tempo, playing inside on her private phonograph, so into it that she actually forgot to take off her clothes; and nobody noticed but just sang along silently or watched a personal movie that was playing in the darkness six inches in front of their eyes, maybe XXX-rated but maybe, quite possibly, very much touchingly not; or drifted off to sleep to some remembered jukebox lullaby.

I was spacing-out myself, when I caught a glance of a dame's face lit from the round window in the kitchen door as she headed off for the corridor that leads to the ladies' room. It was Stella, no doubt about it, unmistakable though looking older than the photograph, or maybe it was just the light. She disappeared down the corridor and I edged my chair around a little and watched the dark nook like a hawk.

A couple of guys had started arguing over the jukebox. Sounded like the one guy wanted to hear a new song, while the other guy, in contradiction to this, wanted to hear the old one again, for like the seventh time. Diplomatically, it appeared to be an impasse. Negotiations started to deteriorate. An unkind opinion was expressed by the first guy, possibly directed at present company (the second guy), concerning whacked-out booze-hounds who wanted to hear the same damned shitkicker music over and over again. A wounding guess was ventured by the party of the second part, concerning the probable sexual orientation of the rock-star that the new guy wished to hear, along with some quite gratuitous animadversions towards possible ancestral irregularities concerning the new guy himself. This exchange piqued the interest of a bunch of other guys, consisting severally of guys who liked rock and hated country-western, guys who enjoyed country-western and deprecated rock, plus guys who either liked or hated (whether based upon actual acquaintance, or general principles) either one of the original guys at the jukebox, plus guys who hated fags and guys who were fags, if any (maybe just some tendencies in that direction, nothing serious; we were drunk, okay?), plus guys who didn't give a shit about any of this but just liked to fight, plus other guys who personally would take a pass on that (this nice new suit) but who enjoyed watching *other* guys fight; and who, by their loud and hearty cries, stirred on the combatants (who by now were many) on to ever greater pinnacles of the pugilistic art; plus even some poor sucker who felt duty-bound to try to break up fights (he got decked right away). Not to mention (among those present) the usual passel of kibitzers and hangers-on, plus people just passing though and pausing momentarily but distracted and not really taking it all in properly, then hurrying on to wherever they had to get off to; and in the outermost circle, cool heads placing side bets, and a silent gliding coterie of the light-fingered, who sensed an opportunity to effect, unobserved, a transfer of wealth to their own advantage.

So there was a fairish amount of physical activity, chairs flying around and splintering glass, and alarums and loud comments such that you might hardly notice the small-caliber pistol shot unless you were a fellow, like myself, trained from infancy to pick up on such subtleties, sitting as I was quite coolly at the bar, every inch the professional, sipping my beer without hurry and keenly observing the goings-on. And what got to me was that the gunshot did not come from inside the crowd of guys duking it out at the far end, but rather from the darkness and from a distance that you couldn't reasonably hope to hit any particular guy in the writhing revolving mass out on the floor. It was as if somebody had a private quarrel off to the side, and this seemed like a good time to settle it.

Some bouncers were ambling up to the free-for-all, pissed about the jukebox which was now on its side although, amazingly, still playing, (and, even more amazingly, playing, not the first guy's song, not the second guy's song, but something entirely different, a slow sad waltz in fact; someone in all the confusion had managed to slip in a nickel); the bouncers (used to this) taking their own sweet time so that the pugilists could burn up some calories and be easier to shoo out the door. Really didn't matter; furniture all destroyed by now anyway. They were concentrating on the action and didn't seem to have noticed the shot. I slid off the barstool and motioned for Joey to follow me. The far darkness I didn't trust, so I circled around by the craps tables where the action was *still* going on undisturbed. Then a woman screamed and the lights went out and I got nervous and started to edge toward the short corridor that led to the rest rooms, but the sporting crowd was now spilling over and I got jostled pretty bad, bleeding, thrown back against the wall. I replied in kind and a fellow tumbled over backwards onto the floor, prompting someone else to seize this opportune moment to stomp the supine figure with a biker's boot and someone else, someone I had absolutely no beef with and didn't know him from Adam, took a swing at me and I moved away, trying to keep my eyes on where she would come out, and wondering bitterly if I'd missed her. Then back in the brouhaha, someone else fell, this time right into the craps table, causing the chips to get all messed in with one another, a complete confusion of Mine and Thine, and instantly you had hands grabbing chips and hands grabbing hands and hands flashing knives — it got so bad that even the quiet and motionless gentlemen drawn in a closed circle around the roulette wheel, which continued to revolve slowly, silently, fatefully through all this, gentlemen who had something riding on red, and who were watching the little silver ball intently as it rattled insanely on the turning wheel, the wheel so smooth and regular and unruffled, the ball like a crazed ferret, hopping this way and that, slipping, back-tracking, never making up its mind where to settle down, until The Wheel, at its own appointed time, as foretold in the Gospels, should eventually come to rest, and the ball at last, if only through sheer exhaustion, lie quietly in just one single slot, its fate now finally decided: even these gentlemen did now look up. Then another gunshot, much louder and closer this time and of a higher caliber, at which point the bouncers figure, *That tears it*, and the saps come out and the jackets come off and they start laying about them every whichway and that, their pent-up energy and the natural animal high spirits of healthy young males now being let out in a most satisfying manner, take *that* take *that*, not caring who got it, bodies everywhere, like a symphony reaching crescendo. I try to shove my way through the swirling mob towards the rest rooms, but someone takes it personal and snaps my head back. My boot finds his groin and his buddies cross me off their Christmas list and come at me with table-legs that earlier proceedings had conveniently separated from the parent tables, or maybe they'd been supplied by management for just such an occasion as this, standing until needed in a sort of umbrella stand at the entrance to the roadhouse. I beat a retreat back towards the roulette table, the sole remaining island of something like sanity in all this, where most of the sadder and wiser heads have turned aside from the Vanity Fair and resumed their intent inspection of the wheel, calmly obedient to the laws of physics, while the jittering ball bows to some other laws, some laws from beneath the earth. I notice the stripper, back in her bathrobe, up on the platform, taking her smoking break all alone on a little folding chair towards the back of the stage, then she looks at her watch and, my my, it's time, it's her time; so she rises and disrobes and walks dreamily to center stage, where she begins to dance and sway, slowly as though in time to the sweet sad waltz, still playing out of the jukebox somewheres beneath the general confusion, though by now you can't hardly hear it.

I am contemplating my next move when a hand, completely unprovoked, emerges out of nowhere and squeezes something painfully sensitive around the neck. I don't say anything, having lost the power of speech, but the eyeballs tell the whole story in a way more eloquent than words, and Joey notices, and calmly picks the guy up bodily and slams him down onto the central spike of the roulette wheel, where he spins like a stuck pig. This, naturally, disappoints the gentlemen who, amidst the sound and fury of the world, had been attempting to attend to their own deeply philosophical spectacle, but by now it's moot anyway because the joint is swarming with cops, both the bought ones and the not bought ones, the bent ones and the not-yet-bent ones, and patrons are searching for their wraps and quickly powdering their noses one last time while deciding to call it a night, only the smoke that had been gathering almost unnoticed turns out to be a fire from the rest-room area where, perhaps, some careless individual had ignored a no-smoking sign, and people are running shouting and screaming every whichway and then something blows up. Then even the cops take a powder and the roof starts falling in, and I head for the doorway with Joey in tow. We leave without leaving a tip.

People are piling into cars and fighting over other cars not yet piled into and even, probably without all warrant, vigorously disputing ownership of vehicles already occupied, at which point I start to worry that someone might hop into mine for lack of other suitable transportation, so we head down the road, Joey and I, ducking the slashing headlights of people peeling out of there both sides of the divider and some on the shoulder and some winding up in a ditch. The high-beams of one hit another car broadside: and like a flash photograph I see Stella, Stella, seemingly calm but pale as death, sitting beside a might-be-Hispanic guy at the wheel. Don't have a camera but my eyes take a perfect photograph, which will yield a soundless still-life of one brief moment of the world's whirl.

We reach our car where this young guy is trying to hot-wire it and we remove him from the vehicle and hit the gas. People are swerving off down side roads, chased by cop cars, or heading down to the beach to escape along the endless sands, or perhaps to just head out into the boundless ocean, now dark and silent and beckoning in its chilling way; and pretty soon we have the road pretty much to ourselves. We're driving along just normally and Joey turns to me and says, "Hey, wow, what was *that* all about?"

I grin with bloodied lips. "I d'know, Joey, but it's a great beginning."

"*Effin'* A-men ta that."

We told Larsen what we had on her so far, basically that she was running with a pretty rough crowd. He seemed concerned but not surprised. He gave me the address of the apartment she had now, and suggested we stake it and tail her. Find out who visits her and what she does with them. And he wanted photographs.

I didn't like that part. "Her I'm not that interested in, " I said, "if it's all the same to you. It's a cinch she's not the muscle, probably not even the brains behind this thing. It's the guys she's in with, maybe against her will. I got a pretty good look at the guy she left with and at the car. I'll ask around and run him down."

He shook his head nix. "You'd just alert them, and then you're a dead man. No, keep to the shadows. Get evidence. We can't beat this outfit head-on but maybe we can sidle around and stymie them. Anyhow your best bet to find the greaser is to stick with her."

I agreed reluctantly. He advanced me some money for film.

Back at the homestead for a dinner of leftover frozen cheese pizza. I said gloomily, "It's come to this."

"Not for long, though," chuckled Joey. "Be a large, fresh from La Mama's, everything on it, plus everything *else* on top of *that*, plus extra anchovies." He pulls out a TV Guide he bought from the change left over from buying the film, window-shopping for when we can buy back the freedom of our TV. "Boy, cartoons, cop shows ... Oh, wow, Murphy, lookit this! A flick on the tube, it's called 'Malibu Madness'! Oooh ... "

"Sound good, huh? Whatsit say ina paper?"

"Oh, they liked it, Murph. Says: 'A great movie if you like endless car chases.' Oh boy, do I!"

The phone rings and I reach for it. I grunt, "Murphy," and a faraway-sounding voice says, "We've warned you. We won't warn you again. Lay off this case." I make a disgusted sound and hang up.

"Who was it, Murphy?" asks Joey, not looking up from the Guide.

"Wrong number."

We staked out the address he'd given us, Joey doing the day shift and me hitting the night. First couple shifts, nothing happens, then the next night I'm in the bushes and she shows up with the same guy. She looks tired but not so scared anymore, and she gives his arm a squeeze as they go up the steps.

I don't like my position but the fact is, curiosity is getting the better of me, wondering what their game is. Cause so far it doesn't make sense. I haven't been able to get inside yet and bug the apartment — fourth floor, no balcony, other tenants coming and going all the time, and a police station right across the street — but I can get an idea of where their heads are at just by snapping them letting them know it. No infrared sight for this job, just a good old-fashioned flash. Heck I oughta stick a press card in my hat.

They're standing framed in the front doorway, the street number clearly visible above it, while she fumbles for her key. She murmurs something like "Raul, dear," ... I somehow didn't want to hear that. I mean it mighta been "bowel" or "trowel" or "foul" or "scowl," only they ain't names.

I step forth from the shadows and carefully press the flash button, filling their faces with sudden light.

They turn, and my second shot catches their look of horror. My third shot catches her escort with his arm across his face, a shield against the light-spitting darkness. I step forward a little more, to see if he'll go for a gun; but my next shot catches him shrinking back, looking sick.

I blow; no sense pressing my luck. He may have friends watching the action from cars. I thread out through an alley and hop into my car — well, the one I been using — where I left it, and drive home slowly, mouth tasting of ash.

"Whacha been up to, m'brother?" Joey asks when he sees my grey face.

"Flashing."

Larsen shuffles the photographs and says grimly, "They're playing hardball."

I say: Say what?

Frowning one eyebrow and pointing with his pen. "That's Raul Benevan. A professional. Contract killer, prefers a knife. What's more, I think they've discovered my escape route."

Say hunh? I sit back and let him tell it.

"Since this whole thing started, I've been keeping an unlisted apartment. I meet my chauffeur in a secluded corner of the executive parking garage. It's guarded, but God knows if I can trust the guard. He drives me home by a roundabout route in a rented car — different car and different trajectory every day. But the last two days, we've been followed — I'm sure of it. And now someone seems to be staking out my apartment. I tell you frankly I'm worried."

Joey made sympathetic noises but I remained silent, still feeling the taste in my mouth.

"You should worry too, Murphy," he says, with an edge to his voice. "If they kill me, you don't get paid."

I tell him okay, I'll look into it, starting tomorrow; but that there's an angle that I have to check out elsewhere tonight. He says okay.

"What's the angle?" asks Joey as we walk down the back stairway.

"The angle is, no angle: I'm going to tail *him*. You take the car and drive home alone — in fact, drive by slowly right under his window, so he can recognize it if he happens to see it, by its banged-in roof. Wait for me at home."

"I don't get it."

"You don't got to. Just get."

I didn't even have to hotwire a car; some guy had left spare keys under the mat in an Olds parked nearby that wasn't hard to get into. I waited by the exec lot exit, and pretty soon I saw him coming out, only no chauffeur, him driving, same car he drove when he first came to see me. Must be varying his routine to throw his pursuers off.

I followed him at a distance that I let get longer and longer because he wasn't making it difficult at all. After ten minutes he double-parks and is buzzed in to an apartment. He comes back down with a broad in a mink.

Dusk is falling. They drive slowly, me tailing them, and nobody else tailing so far's I can tell. They stop at some swank apartments, and Larsen gives his car to a doorman, then lets himself and the mink lady in with a key. I'm starting to think I have his number when I notice a tiny flash of light on the roof of the two-storey across the street. It could be nothing. Or it might mean a lot.

I head around back of it through an alley and shinny up to the fire escape, creep up it and flatten myself against a ventilation duct on the roof. There's the guy all right, with a lit cigarette, half-hidden. Must've been the lighting of it that blew his game. Shouldn't smoke when you're on the job, dope. (Shouldn't drink either, maybe, but hey, that's different.)

I edge forward. A lamp is on in Larsen's apartment building that wasn't on before he went in. It's on the third floor, just opposite the guy on the roof. A woman's figure passes before the uncurtained window, then is joined by a man. The roof guy kneels, aims. It's not Raul and it's not a knife he's wielding. Guy's got a goddam telescopic sight.

I'm on him in a flash and we're rolling around on the gravel and tarpaper. Before things have even got serious, he grunts and goes limp — I must have winded him somehow. I stand up, hold him down with my boot, then crouch and pat his pockets for further weapons but there's nothing. He lifts his head and says, disgustedly, "You idiot. Do you have any idea what that camera cost?"

I go over and, sure enough, a smashed camera, fancy job with a telephoto. He stands up, dusting himself off and cursing. But what I got now ain't no camera, it's a .45 and it's pointed straight at his navel. I bark at him, "You got ten seconds to tell me who's behind it and when is the hit for, or your guts are gonna be liver paste all over that wall."

He shakes his head in disbelief. "Who the hell are you?" And then he gets it. "You working for *Larsen*?"

For some reason the question is embarrassing, but I'm not gonna let him stall for time. "It's now down to eight seconds and you're gonna get it where ya don't want it if you don't come across."

He rolls his eyeballs. "Oh, I don't be-lieeeve this. Look, *she* hired me, okay? His wife, Stella. A man's gotta eat. But this I don't need. — Look, forget it. A hundred a day, this ain't worth it to me. I quit. You want my client? She's all yours. Go ahead, work for *both* of them, sure why not, get it coming and going, both sides of the street. *I* don't care; be my guest."

He bends down and I tense, suspecting a trap — "No funny stuff! (hands tightening on the grip) — but he just picks up his hat and walks off. I am left all alone on the roof.

Head swimming, eyes smarting; the gun sinks. I stare at it like what is it even doing there. I wince, rub my forehead, and climb slowly back down.

I drove the found car back to where I found it, leaving an unsigned note saying sorry for the mixup plus a couple of dollars in the glove compartment for the gas. Then I took a taxi home.

Joey meets me at the door and he's all excited. "Lookit this, Murphy, it was nailed by a dagger to our door!" He hands me a crude circle, cut from black construction paper. Inscribed in blood-red crayon: *Lay off this case.*

"Yeh, great, Joey, thanks. Look, I'm kind of tired. I'm turning in."

Larsen's next idea is that we bug her phone.

I sigh okay and we set it up. That evening brings the following conversation:

"Hello?"

"Darling."

"Raul! My sweet."

"Stella. Darling."

"I've been worried. Things have been so strange."

"Don't worry, darling, I'll be right over. And I've got some Kind Bud for you."

"Fine, good," she says wearily. "Come on over. It'll help me relax."

And then some mushy stuff that I wouldn't repeat it, in mixed or unmixed company. Anyhow it's all on tape.

I go back with what I got.

Joey is very interested in this. "The drug angle, huh! Always does turn up, sooner or later, when the Syndicate's in the picture. I'll scout around, keep my ear to the ground, maybe call in some markers, see if the city's getting ready for a big shipment. Maybe those two are taste-testers for the shadowy buyer — Mr. Big."

Larsen turns out to be interested too. At his suggestion, I break into her car and swipe a scarf of hers. He sends it to a lab and they find traces of marijuana particles. "A bad business," he says, repressing a smile.

At home, the hotplate's on the fritz, and we're eating cold beans out of a can. But it could be caviar, would make no difference. Everything's tasting of ash.

Joey's feeling pumped, though. "Not much longer of this, good brother! Like they say in the comics: Victory is Nigh."

He sets the TV Guide down with about half the things circled, then notices I don't say anything, and he gives me a concerned look. "I dunno, Murphy, this job tonite, you sure you want to shadow them alone? We're getting close to where they live, Murph, their higher-ups I mean. Your life ain't worth a split nickel if they spot you in the nightclub."

"No, thanks, that's okay. Look, how about you stay home and make sure, ah, nobody plants any TNT in our refrigerator."

"Jeepers! Never thought of that. You go to a fridge for a cold one, and it's all wired up, and, BLAM! Last beer you'll ever have. — Actually worse than that, account of the blam comes before the beer. You die thirsty. What a scummy outfit these guys are! — Good thinking, Murphy, I'm on it."

The breeze is blowing through the kitchen window, gently stirring the pale faded curtains, and just then a rock comes sailing in. It lies on the floor, with a note wrapped around it. Joey eyes it nervously like it might be a bomb.

I stare at it. "Something's fishy here, Joey. These are the wimpiest hoods I ever heard of. I mean, these little *notes*, a black *spot*? Who are we, the Hardy Boys?"

I unwrap the note. It says: *Your final warning.*

I crush it up and fling it in the can, feeling nothing but self-disgust. "See you later, Joey," and go.

I arrived early at the club where I knew they had reservations, since they'd made them from her phone. The ash stayed dry despite beer after beer, it just could not be washed away. But I was in it this far, and I had to play the hand to the end.

They took a banquette in the corner like I figured they would, not twelve feet from my own table. They held hands, and he put a tiny velvet-covered box up on the table. For a while they said nothing, gazing into each other's eyes. But at last he leaned forward, and kissed her on the lips: their faces lit only by candlelight, but it was enough for the fast film I had in the camera hidden on my lap.

The next day I called up Larsen and told him what I had. He said fine, put it all together and he'd come by to pick it up. "I'm bringing a check."

"Mm. See. So the case is over."

"Ye-es, thank you, Mr. Murphy, thanks to both of you. You've done quite enough."

"Yeh. And that tail and the stakeout still bothering you?"

"What? Oh — that. No, no; I seem to have given them the slip."

He was over at our place in twenty minutes, nodded in satisfaction at the latest tapes and photographs.

"Fine, this is fine. Anything else?"

Joey frowned. "Actually not all that much. The way I had this situation figured, a case this big, I thought there would be more."

He smiled and waved away our cares. "That's fine, it doesn't matter. This should be quite enough." He locked the evidence in an attaché case, then laid a freshly-cut cashier's check smoothly down upon the table. Joey picked it up and his eyes got wide. "Jeez, thanks. Ya didden hafta — "

Our employer heads out the door and I'm biting my lip. He goes down the stairs, clomp clomp, and now he's laughing: bursting out into the sunlight, laughing louder now. His laughter echoes up and down, up and down the empty street. Joey looks at me quizzical like What's up. I motion him over to the window.

There he is at the curb, getting into a big black limousine. The chauffeur's hands are on the wheel; he is wearing one black glove.

Joey goes still, then starts tearing down the stairs. I stumble after him. We hit the sidewalk just as the car is pulling away from the curb. And it pauses, and the chauffeur turns around to look us up and down. And it's him, the scarface, giving us the same hideous hellish grin. Then he guns it, pulling away, the throaty roar of the powerful engine drowning out their laughs.

Goddam divorce case after all.

Joey looks sadly down at the check, tears it slowly into little strips. I feel bad at being had, but he must feel worse, this whole thing having been partly his idea; plus the disappointment of not getting back the TV. I go and I put an arm around his shoulder.

Joey manages a weak smile, and then a better smile, then simply shrugs.

"*It's* all right, Murphy." He gives my shoulder the old squeeze. "Anyhow, there's nothing good on."

~ The End ~

MURPHY'S THEORY OF COSMOLOGY

One thing, you gotta hand it to the Universe: It — Is— Big. Seriously big.

Bigger'n all get-out —

like, yea-ea-ea big ...

You know the old song, "So high, you can't get over it — So low, you can't get under it — So wide, you can't get around it." Well that's the universe, right down to the ground.

I read somewhere, where the universe, it's already this big, but now it's blowing up even bigger, like a balloon. I mean, what's *that* about?

Anyhow, my theory is — we're guests here — it's like a campsite, sposta leave it nicer than you found it. So, bottom line: Don't cuss; try not to do too much bad stuff; and for you married guys? — always leave the toilet seat down.

SORRY ABOUT THAT

So it's a normal day, and we're sittin' around, only...

"Wanna shoot some pool, Murphy?"

"Nah, Joey. I'm too dipress'."

"Go score a pizza?"

"No, Joey, no appetite."

Joey frowns.

"Maybe pick up some broads?"

"Sorry, good brother, I'm just not'na mood."

Now they say, the thing they say is, you be down so low you think you hit bottom, only thing cheer you up's a guy gone lower'n you. So just then we hear a moan, floating up the stairwell, and then this h-h-r-rrrr *thunk*, h-h-r-rrrr *thunk*, like somebody's dragging himself up the stairs.

Now I know, a case like that, you oughta go help out the guy, or at least shout encouragement from the top of the stairs, but Joey and me were just like frozen to our chairs. It was just so amazing, that steady sound, low but coming closer and closer. And pretty soon, soon enough for us anyways, in slithers this old man.

Hard to tell how old, actually, but his hair all whichways and his face all streaked, crawling along on two elbows and one patched knee, other leg just dragging along like it's dead. Dark glasses with round lenses, like the blind guys wear.

"So what's new, grandpa?" I say, just to break the ice.

He moans, says like he's talking to himself, "I just knew something bad would happen today."

Now me, I'm a detective, just like the sign outside says: "Murphy Brothers — Private Investigators — Discretion Assured." And a detective, he likes to know how a guy knows what he says he knows. So I say: "And just how did you just know that?"

"It's the anniversary of my mother's death, just one year to the day."

"Oh, uh, sorry to hear it." I shift around on my seat but none of it's comfortable anymore. "Course, we all gotta go sometime. Me I'm just tryina make it through the *day*."

"Yes," he sighed, "we all have to go, but not *that* way."

"What way?"

"Eaten by dogs."

He wiped away a tear. Oo-oh ... I feel like I gotta say something. "How'd your old man take it?"

"My father? I never knew him. Nor did she."

"Oh! I ... Oh I, uh ... Unh. So what happen today?"

Again the sigh. "Some ruffians, they stole my crutch."

Oh, oh, oh. I'm practicly starting to feel sorry for the guy. "How'd it happen?"

"I was just setting out to walk the seventeen miles across town to go visit my daughter in the crippled children's home, when they set upon me, beat me, went through my pockets and, finding nothing but a pre-war subway token, no longer valid, I keep it for luck, though it has never worked, in a rage of frustration stole my crutch out of spite."

Joey looked indignant, me I was getting choked up. The man went on.

"My only consolation is that I could tell by the sound where they disappeared to. I know where their hideout is. They suspect nothing."

"All *right*, pops!" I said, jumping out of my chair. "Don't you worry. We'll get it back for you. Just show us the way."

He nodded, wiped at his eye again, and through the dust you could almost make out a smile. "Thank you, son, thank you."

He handed us a slip of paper on which he'd written an address. I looked at it and grimaced. Funky part of town. "You got it, pops."

Then he put in, low and cautiously: "You'll have to be careful. They'll have guns."

I scoffed and thumped my chest. "We got guns, we got guts, we got smarts. They're dead men."

This time he couldn't suppress a smile. "I don't know how to thank you young men. You know I have nothing to pay you with — well, except these shoes. You could have them. One of them does me no good anyway."

The other one neither, the shape they're in, but I wave it away. "No problem, pops, it's on the house. Say, how'd you get that game leg anyway?"

Again he heaved a mighty sigh. "I was just coming back from the funeral, where they buried my only son. Bent over with grief, I wandered into traffic. It was my own fault and I blame myself. A limousine clipped me and I had no medical coverage so the leg just died."

I shook my head. "Gee, that's rough. You know it suprises me though, you bein' a poor man, how good you talk."

"Ye-es," he said, tilting his head back. "I used to be a surgeon, back in the old days. That was before I lost my sight ..."

"Whew! Okay look, you just sit tight, y'hear? Just rest your bones till we get back. We're gonna do the deed."

Fact of the matter, we exaggerated a little about those guns. Business is been kind of slow lately, and the only one we got is in hock. But these guys sounded like a bunch of punks and we figured we wouldn't need one. Anyhow you don't shoot some guys just cause they stole a crutch, rotten as that is. So we swung round their clubhouse, basement job with windows at sidewalk level all crusted with sidewalk dust, but you wipe it aside and you can peer in. I couldn't believe it. If this was the Dead End Kids it was after graduation, or a senior auxiliary or something, because there were about ten of them in their twenties and looked to be thirties, standing around and sitting around and a big pile of money on the card table they got. Guns everywhere — Lugers, rifles, sawed-offs, what looked like a Uzi off in a corner, but there it was, leaning against the boiler, a crutch. "Jeez, Joey, I don't know," I said, standing up stiffly. "Look like we bite off more'n we can chew."

"Won't be the first time, Murphy. Want to let the cops go get it?"

"What is this, Joey? You been out ina sun too long? Cops go by the cost, cost to them and price tag ona goods. A crutch, that's petty cash, no way a felony, probly not even a misdemeanor. They're not gonna risk their heads get shot off for that. They be more interested in our parking tickets, pay for the whole Policeman's Ball. Plus those guys look like they're payin' protection, just all out practicly in the open like that. No, we gotta put our heads together."

No guns, but we got smarts in spades, I figure. I go rummage round the trunk, see what we got, we got some smoke bombs left over from the Fourth. So we tool around to the projects, half the apartments empty but they still got smoke alarms, only now they don't. So we fill up the trunk with those and drive back to the clubhouse. There we divvy up the goods. Joey ducks down the areaway and finds the fuse box for the building. I wait by the windows, he waits down below by the door.

Heck, for the Murphys, a thing like this it's a piece of cake.

One ... two ... three ... Joey hits the fuses and the basement goes dark. I smash the windows and he kicks in the door. We each toss in some smoke bombs and an armload of smoke-alarms. You can't even hear them saying "What th — ?!" cause the place is going crazy. It's like twenty fire engines all screaming through the basement, plus some of the guys are shooting but they don't know what at. I figure if anyone's got his head up he'll guard the long green on the table; meanwhile I just scoop up the crutch. But when I get to it, some bozo's got his hands on it, can you feature that? So I had to deck him. We light out of there with the crutch and the wise guys don't even see us, they're just bounding around down there in the dark, shooting and cursing and raising Cain. We jump in the Chrysler where it's waiting with its engine running, and peel out of there laying rubber all over the road.

We're still whooping when we get back to the homestead and go clattering up the stairs. "Boy," says Joey, "I wish I coulda seen the 'xpressions on their faces," he says.

"You'd'a seen their expressions they'd'a seen yours and you' d be dead," I say. "Anyhow we got it."

We barge into the room and the old guy's sitting up now, looking better, looking not quite so old. When he sees the crutch he licks his lips.

"You done good, boys," he says, and his voice is hoarser than before. "Now give me that and I'll just be running along — "

But Joey doesn't even hear him, he's so revved up he's waving the crutch and doing a little end-zone victory dance. "Man you shoulda seen how we faked out those suckers," he whoops.

I'm starting to murmur "I thought you —", but no-one's listening to me either.

"Man we come on like ghostbusters," he says, and he jigs over to the pool table where the balls are already racked, a neat triangle the kind you love to bust up. He hefts the crutch like a cue. "We had'em right where we want'em and we zap'em like — that!" *Wham* he sends the cue ball into the rack and scatters them every whichway. A wild shot but he sinks three balls. Only, with the blow, the cap on the end of the crutch falls off.

"Gee, sorry," says Joey, looking down.

And then he keeps looking down. Out onto the pool table are rolling diamonds, emeralds, who knows what all they are: red guys and green guys and white guys and sparklies, rolling on out of the hollow crutch. I'm staring at it. I been trying to put two and two together but now there's this and this and this and this and the numbers are whirling around in my eyeballs like fruit in a slot machine. But the old guy, he doesn't miss a beat, he hops right over and his glasses are off and he's smiling and he's got a gun. "Clumsy of you but we'll let it ride," he says, packing the sparklies back in with his left hand and stuffing some into his pockets. "I'm much obliged to you both."

Joey's dumbfounded, then he finds his voice. "Hey you ..."

"I know," he smiles, dismissing our surprise with a wave of his hand. "It's a sight to make the lame walk and restore vision to the blind. Over a million in ice and most of it no longer even traceable. Be a long story, and I told enough stories for today. Well, it's been nice knowing you boys," as he backs out, the re-capped crutch under his left arm and keeping us covered with the gun. But he don't have to bother, I got no fight left, I'm just standing there feeling like I never been born. In the doorway, he hesitates. "Why the long faces, pal?" But I don't say a thing, my head's just hanging down. He gives a little nervous laugh. "Hey look, them's the breaks, don't take it so hard."

It's like I can't even hear him, just drowning, down, drowning, I'm feeling so bad. "He-hey-y-y ... Oh, heck. Here," and from out of his pocket he tosses me a pearl the size of an egg. "It's a tip. You earned it."

Then he exits and disappears from our life. I catch it automatic, now I'm staring at it like I don't know what it is. Joey whistles. "Some pearl, Murphy."

I stare at it and slowly I scowl at it and then I say, real bitter, "Yeh let's see what it's good for."

I toss it on the pool table and I grab a cue and I hit it hard, *hard*, like I'm mad so bad I can taste it.

Then maybe it was fake, or maybe deep down inside the shininess it had a hidden fault, some inside rottenness; or maybe I just don't know my own strength. Anyway it shattered into about sixteen hundred pieces. Just dust.

Joey's eyes bug out, then he settles back and kind of relaxes. "Maybe just as well, Murphy. No good ever come of a thing like that."

He shakes his head, looking at the fragments all over the pool table and me standing there with a cue. Then he grins. "Y' know, you sure are a hoot, though, Murphy."

And in spite of it all I sort of see the humor of it. "Yeh, y'know, this whole day's been weird."

Now the grin goes all out. "Say, you're lookin' a little better, there, Murph."

I manage a dry chuckle. "Yeh, you know, for a while there what I thought was, whoever it is watches over Murphy went and sent that guy to buck me up, me feeling low and him being lower, then it turns out he's a millionaire."

Joey splays his hands out and his face expands like it's gonna fill the whole room. "But that's it, Murphy, don't you see it? He is, he's low, low as you can go. You wouldn't want to be in his shoes even after he changes back into his Guccis. Cos see, *that* guy, what he done, he's gonna French-fry forever. But you'n me, we it least got a chance a checkin' in to that Big Hotel."

"Hm, hope so. Course, He'll be pretty pissed when He sees us."

"Ah heck, we may have to pay some dues, don't worry about it, they got a place for that, they got it all worked out. Heck even *that* guy might scrape by when he gets right down to it, looked like his doorway towards the end there was open just a crack."

I give him a little love-punch on the shoulder. "C'mon, man, I just worked up a appetite."

I scrounge around in my pocket, "Got just enough for a plain pizza."

He digs in his. "I got for the topping."

"Anchovies!"

"You said it!"

"An'after that I'll playya a pool."

"Great! An'after that ..."

We head out the doorway.

"Y'know, Joey, this is shapin' up to be a really great day."

~ *The End* ~

Murphy: DE THEOLOGIA

She let out a silent stream of smoke. "Go on."

"Well." Murphy shifted on the couch. "See my Dad wasn't around none, nobody to keep me in line. And my Mom — she was just busy, I guess. So not too much church stuff ..."

Her face registered alarm.

"No no no — no sweat," he continued. "I did get baptized, they did take care of that. — But yeh, hey — wouldn't that be embarrassing. You're shuffling along in line at the Pearly Gates, they ask to see your baptismal certificate; you're like, slapping your pockets — Dang! Must of left it in the other suit!"

WATCH THE BIRDIE

[First appeared in *Alfred Hitchcock Mystery Magazine*, June 1988]

So this one time, I'm sittin' at the window, lookin' out over the lean streets. Nothing shaking; nothing moves. The sun slants down, gets just a little bit inside the canyon of the alleys, slops all over the sidewalks, hottens up the asphalt. And then a cloud passes over the sun.

I'm looking down, and I see a man, walking through the wrong part of town.

He takes a step, stops; looks around, moves forward, stops again. He looks down at the sidewalk, holds his chin. He wheels around, takes two steps, then he freezes, and spins back. He walks past my building, hesitates in front of the entrance, goes on, and then I lose him, 'count of the angle. But then he reappears coming back the other way, hesitates again, and goes in. Then I hear his footsteps coming up the stairs.

I straighten my T-shirt and get ready for a customer. He must be coming to me, cause all the other rooms are empty.

He appears in the open doorway, stops, and stares at me. I wave him in.

He's well-dressed, all right, better than I realized through the streaky window. Dark suit, black shined shoes — little dusty, maybe, from walking up and down in the earth. I glance down at my beer-stained T-shirt, my cords with the dog-turd cuffs, then I realize that's not what he's staring at. He's looking me right in the eye.

"Name?" he says, and I say, "Murphy," then do a double-take. He just come in here, and it's like *he's* the one sitting at the desk.

"Your sign says P.I."

"The sign does not lie."

"Can I trust you?"

"You'll have to."

"You're right."

He frowns, and bites his lip, like the idea is new to him, and he starts pacing in my office. Nervous guy.

But then he turns on me and says, with perfect self-control, "I need you to find a man."

I lean back in my chair and spread my hands. "Bread and butter to me; What's he done?"

"Drugs. Guns. And done it big."

I shrug. "So go to the police."

He snorts. "You know them as well as I do, in this town. Anyhow this case has a twist. The man's a diplomat, a foreign national. We're not sure how he fits in. But if we can prove he's here, we can get him on a visa violation — he's not posted to here. The whole thing's very delicate. Wheels within wheels. We can't say at this point just who-all is involved. Maybe the Eurotrash bad guys — maybe ... Mr. Big. But you bring the local cops in, they'll be treading on the flowerbeds in no time."

"So what about the Federals?"

"We get enough evidence, they'll come in. But right now all we have are some tips and some leads, some guesses and hunches, and a funny new pattern in the international traffic. You verify the suspect, things'll start falling into place."

"Hm. Still ... something's fishy about this. You say he's pushing dope. Okay. By me, he can get his. But how do I know this isn't just a personal thing; like, I find him, then you rub him out?"

"Because you *let him go*. You got that? It's not *him* we want specifically, it's the whole network, and he can lead us to it. All I need is a photo proving he's in this country, and the Feds take care of the rest. After you find him — you got some delicate conscience, there, mister — after that, you can *wait*, if you want, forty-eight hours, whatever, suit yourself, until you tell me: time enough for him to blow CONUS. Sound good?"

"Guess so. So where do *you* fit in?"

His face hardens a little. "I'm with Interpol. We've been tracking this case for a year."

I got nothing else on the docket and it sounds like it could be interesting. I say, "I'll take the case."

He relaxes some and sits down.

"Your name?"

"Jeffers. Maurice Jeffers."

"His name?"

"That's what we don't know."

"You have a photo of him?"

"Unfortunately not."

"Description?"

"Almost certainly a diplomat."

"Yeh but, yeh but, I mean, is he *tall*? short? dark, fat, what? Distinguishing marks, facial hair, and all that?"

"Mr. Murphy, you're missing the point. We don't have a picture, just a frame. We know the country he's coming from, we think we know what his game is, but we don't know who. He is 'X', the unknown in the equation. We have the equation. You solve for X."

"X, huh. And you want me to find him."

"Right."

"X. Look. I think I'm missing a lot of things. I mean, I got guys come in here, want me to find someone disappeared over a year ago. Dames, want me to find their hubby what they ain't seen since breakfast. Find someone who turns out he's already dead. Find someone turns out he lives only in their head. *Eck* setera, *eck* setera. But you, you won't even tell me what he looks like, what his name is. Nothing."

"Something. I can tell you this." The stranger leans forward like a conspiracy. "He has a love interest here in town. I think I know who it is. Stake her out, he'll walk into the trap."

Now it's me who's pacing.

"And the dame, what, she would be like — *Y*?"

He cracks half a smile. "No, her we have a little more on. The name we're not sure, though if she's using an alias that wouldn't be hard to find out. But that's unimportant. What's important is we have an address, the apartment where she keeps her love nest; and this is where Mr. X might come."

He hands it to me, neatly typed.

"Not a bad address," I say. "She's got money. Or her husband does, or her boyfriends, or whatever."

"That doesn't matter. What we do know is that, when she meets her men, she does it mostly mid-afternoons."

"Hm, sounds like she's married, or they are. Hey, though, this love nest used by any other broads? 'Cause I'd hate to be photographing the wrong guy."

"I don't know who else may use it; all the Bureau told me was the address and what I told you. But they did wire a photograph. Quality's not too good, I'm afraid, but it's enough to tell you if you see someone else in there and it's not her. And you'll be seeing her in the flesh soon enough."

I study the photograph. A blonde, very tasty-looking, even in the smudgy black and white. Too bad she's poisoned bait.

"I'll get right on it," I say. "Give me a phone where you can be reached."

"That won't be necessary," he says. "I'll be in touch."

I drive around her neighborhood a while, get a sense of what the target will be walking into. Memorizing the lights, the blocked streets, the one-ways, case I got to get out of there fast. If the guy's big in drugs and gun-running, chances are he'll be packing a gat. I want identification, not confrontation.

The apartment building itself is beautiful but bad news. Takes up a whole small block next to a park, and has entrances on all four sides. It looks like I'm going to have to catch him smack in her apartment. Come to think of it, I'd have to at least spot him there anyway, if I was to know who I'm looking for. Otherwise I'd have to just photograph every one of the dozens of people who went in and out of there every day, at every entrance, gotta be four of me, and do it round the clock, and if I missed even one, that might've been him.

Worse, I'd have to actually photograph him in there when I spot him. 'Cause otherwise he might go out a different exit from the one I was covering, or hang around and not leave till dark, and he might not be back.

After all he's a foreign national, might just be here on a quick trip and not be back for a month or more.

First problem is to locate 3G.

It's a security apartment, you need a key to get in the building or else someone buzzes you up. You can always get buzzed in on some pretext or other, or follow on the heels of someone opening the door, but sometimes the party gets suspicious and alerts a guard. I want a low-low profile on this deal.

Opportunity comes early. A pizza truck stops outside the building and a guy gets out with a box. He goes over to the rank of buzzers and looks down at the box where the address and apartment number are written in pencil. I step forward. "Buzzer's on the fritz, so I came down to get it. What do I owe you?"

"Twelve bucks."

Oh good. Sounds like everything on it.

I pay him and tip him and he drives away. Why should he give it a second thought? Guy pays you for the pie as ordered, standing outside the locked entrance, must be the right guy and must have a key. And I do, but it's not the metal kind.

I buzz the number on the box, 7B. "Pizza delivery." It crackles back, "About time! Come on up." The plate makes a noise like a cicada and I open the door.

I keep the pizza with me, case anyone sees me prowling around, and wonders about the unfamiliar face. Most faces are unfamiliar in these apartment places but I like the insurance. I add a couple little hooks to the penciled number and now it reads 3B. My ticket to the third floor.

It's big. The units on each floor use up most of the alphabet. I swing around and find 3G. It's on the side toward the park.

A party passes and looks at me with mild interest. I wear my moron look and stare down at the apartment number on the box. The party disappears into an elevator and I'm alone.

Hey, great idea. A "G" looks a lot like a "B," especially if you never got past the first few grades. If she's not in, I use my little open-sesame kit and case her apartment. If she's in ...

She is, responding almost immediately to my soft knock. I'm kind of taken aback. Get the act together fast.

"Your pizza, ma'am. Twelve dollars, please."

She looks at me with surprise and distaste at being bothered for nothing. "I didn't order one."

I hook my head around like I'm looking at the metal numbers on the door that swung back, but really taking in the room beyond. "Isn't this 3G?"

"Yes ..." Now she's craning her neck, trying to read the number upside down on my box. "But what you want is 3B."

"Oh, gosh, my bad. I'm sorry," I say. Then she gives a little laugh and says, "Me too." Cause by this time the rich smell of cheese and sausage and tomato sauce all the rest is working its magic, and she's wishing she'd ordered one. I get another idea.

"You know I thought it said 'B'; you never can tell with Paco's scrawl — he's the guy that handles orders to the kitchen. Or hey, it's okay, it's just me I'm like blind. But when I tried it, no one was home."

She looks startled. "Then how'd he ring you in?"

Good thinking. I match it with one of my own, like in checkers. "He didn't. I just followed in behind another delivery man."

She looks thoughtful. "So it could be anyone on this floor."

"Well, or any floor. Maybe the 'B' is right and the '3' isn't."

She laughs again at my plight, and my hapless look.

"You do have a problem. You can't go knocking on every door in the building. It'll get cold. And ... in fact, you're better off not knocking at any wrong doors. Really, you delivery people have a pretty hard job. I'm — sorry I almost snapped at you earlier, but there have been some burglaries, and the building has got awfully security-conscious. More than we have a right to, really; if you think about it, it's kind of self-centered, and selfish. But it sort of rubs off on everybody. The suspicion, the fear. Some of the women especially, they're worried about burglary and — worse. Some of the tenants might greet you at their doorway with a gun."

Her saying "gun" brings me back to my senses. She seems so nice I'd almost forgotten I was dealing with the floozie of a drug kingpin and international arms smuggler. So I hush up my conscience and push the fraud another notch.

"Just my rotten luck," I say with my most crestfallen expression. "Well, it won't be the first time."

Her face melts. "Do they dock you for it?"

"Half the price of the pie."

"That isn't fair! It was the fault of the man who wrote the order."

"Well, not necessarily. The caller might've said it wrong, or said it right but they had a bad connection. Plus the boss takes half the loss."

"Well, I tell you what I'm going to do," she says, determined. "I was just thinking of supper myself, and a pizza sounds scrumptious. What did you say, twelve?"

"Aw, heck, it's pretty cold by now. You can have it for free."

"That's nice of you, but you know you'd still be out six dollars, because your employer is expecting twelve."

I sort of squint up my eyes, then nod, like I'm just figuring it, I'm not too bright.

"Come right in," she says. "Put it, oh ... on the coffee table." And she gives me twelve bucks plus a tip.

"Gee, thanks a lot. You got a microwave? It's not too bad heated up."

I know she doesn't because I already noticed this apartment doesn't come with a kitchen. Either she eats all her meals out or she doesn't need a kitchen 'cause she's only here occasionally, for the trysts.

"No, I ..." she stammers. "But it will be all right."

I thank her and touch my head where the hat would be, and then she laughs again. "I don't know what I'm going to do with all this pizza," she says. "I eat so little."

"It's a large."

She looks at me thoughtfully.

"Do you get yours free?"

"Are you kidding?! The boss we got? Pay the same price as any other customer."

That does it for her. Firmly: "Here. Join in." So I sit on her sofa and share the meal.

It sort of sticks in my throat.

I keep thinking of another guy that broke bread with this other guy that he'd already sold out. But I keep reminding myself that she's the moll of some hardened pusher and gun-runner who's probably ordered about a dozen guys killed. I bite down hard on the crust.

"My, you *are* hungry," she says, with laughing eyes.

From where I sit, I can see the bedroom, and if I weren't here on false pretenses and if I didn't know she was hooked up with a killer, I'd be wondering what we'd both look like in there. She's dressed modestly, but everything she's wearing is so soft you just ache to stroke it. I'm feeling more and more like a heel.

As though reading my thoughts, she colors slightly. "My mother would just die if she knew I let a strange man in. But then, she'd just die if she knew I was here." She colors deeply and hangs her head.

"I — I — I'm sorry, I — "

"No, no," she says, looking up, her eyes a little misty. "It is I who should apologize for embarrassing you, you good person, you decent man. I mean, the way you stuck up for Paco, and, and thought of the loss, the trivial loss incurred by your tight-fisted boss ... Oh!

135

Don't ever let anyone look down on you because you're just a delivery man, because — oh I'm sorry about that 'just,' no, it's wonderful what you do. I mean, it's a clean, honest living you make, bringing food to people who are hungry."

By this point my soul, like some slime-dwelling amphibian exposed to the light, has shriveled into a tiny ball.

"Because there are some people," she says, putting her hand on my wrist, "who earn a much 'better' living in a much worse way. I know," she adds bitterly, "from personal experience."

So it's true! Her boyfriend's a gun-runner, a dealer of drugs.

And she's regretting it! I can't help it, I just burst out:

"L-*lady* ... *Miss* ... *Ma'am* ... Why don't you leave him? Go straight!"

She hangs her head. "How can I, when he's my husband?"

"Your — *husband*?" This is worse than I thought. Really, I have no answer here. My head is swimming. I say something, just to stall for time. "You could — separate."

"And live on what? He wouldn't give me a cent. I have no training for work."

I don't believe in divorce. But ...

Again as if reading my mind. "And he'd never grant me a divorce — unless on terms so prejudicial he could get away with little or no alimony. He needs what he has to support his mistress, and to pay his gambling debts."

Boy, this guy is sounding worse all the time.

Just then the buzzer sounds from downstairs. She speaks mutedly into the mouthpiece:

"Yes?" A muffled reply. She buzzes him in.

"You'd better go now," she says, a note of sorrow in her voice; almost of distress. "I don't know why I told you all this. Just your honest face, and the fact that you're a stranger, and the need for anonymous confession. You don't know me, you know nothing about me, not even my name, and you'll pass from my life ..." She gives me a chaste parting kiss on the cheek, and says, "*I am sorry for what I have done.*"

I step out the door; and as I do, I hear her murmur to herself: "But there can be no forgiveness, for I am doing it again."

My face is burning as I walk back to the elevator. The kiss stings. At least it was her who kissed me and not vice versa — reminds me too much of that guy who kissed the guy.

I push the button for the elevator but it opens immediately and a man steps out. Middle-aged, medium build, an ordinary face. You'd never know it, to look at him ... I watch, standing stock-still in the elevator, as he goes to 3G and knocks.

The elevator sinks, and me with it. How could she marry a guy like that? Maybe she had no idea what he does; you can't read it right off his face. Looks decent enough, if you didn't know better. I hate what I have to do now, but in a way it is almost a favor to her.

They'll identify him and send him upriver. Then she'll be free.

I go to the car and get the camera. Being inside gave me a good layout of the place. They'll probably draw the curtains before they do anything, even though there are no windows facing others and they overlook the park, but I could see the midline where the drapes don't quite meet, and beyond it a tree.

The park is empty, the bushes are thick, the treetops dense with leaves. I shinny up and position myself out on a branch, just a few feet away from her window.

It is not a pretty position to be in. I feel like one of those slime ball peepers. I gotta keep telling myself this is for a good cause. You don't catch Al Capone by just asking him please to come clean.

The drapes are drawn, but the windows are open, and I can hear them talk. Well, hear *her*. His voice is subdued, hers distraught.

" ... it's just, the incredible dishonesty ..." and then her voice falls. Her dress passes by the chink in the drapes.

" ... real estate, they should call it *unreal* estate, this incredible *shell* game ..." She passes by the other way, and this time she's not wearing a dress.

His hand goes up, holding a cigarette, then stubs it out.

She lies down full-length on the bed, perfect view, and reflexively I get a shot of her, top to bottom, though he isn't in the picture yet. Then he lies down on top of her and there's just his back.

The next twenty minutes are among the worst in my life. That's how long it takes to get a decent photo of him, or enough decent partial views to piece together into one man. They'd turned off the overhead lights and there was only the lamp on the nightstand. I snap and snap as their bodies roll in and out of shadow, getting a sliver here, a sliver there, more when the breeze would part the curtains.

Finally they just lie there, unmoving. I climb down, stiff, drenched with sweat and self-disgust. Then I pull back with some establishing shots, to prove where the apartment really is: the window; the window and the wall; the building; the building and a street sign; the street. After all, it won't help the visa people if he's just photographed fornicating somewhere in France.

I get back to my apartment and the phone rings almost instantly, like it knew I was there. I answer, and my voice is hoarse.

"How'd it go?" he says, sounding jolly.

"I got the goods." I wonder if I sound as rotten as I feel.

"Fine, fine, I'll be right over."

He's as good as his word.

He checks through the photographs, one by one down the stack, smiling wryly and sometimes pausing and chuckling over one. My ears burn.

"It's the best I could do. He had his back to the lamp, his face was half in shadow the whole time. And here he had his hand up; and here he's buried in her hair. Good enough if you already know him, I guess, but not the best stuff for Interpol if he's not who they thought and they're trying to pick out a suspect out of a pool of possibles covering two continents."

"It'll do fine," he says, smiling, handing me a check. "It's quite clear enough to show he isn't me."

The world goes dark. I freeze in my tracks. "Isn't *you*? Whadaya mean? I mean — "

"And the photo is really excellent of my wife."

"Of your *wife*?!?!"

"Yes. Thanks for your help, Mr. Murphy. This should stand up just fine in court."

He's put on his hat and he's walking out the door, and I'm — stumbling after him, weeping, and screaming at him, tearing up the check.

"What is this? What **is** *this*? I don't do divorce cases! *I don't do divorce cases!*"

"You just done one," he says.

~ *The End* ~

MURPHY ON MARRIAGE

The mob boss shoots his cuffs, admires the diamond cufflinks, then says casual:

"Y'know ... I'm thinkina marryin' that broad ... Whaddaya think?"

Murphy stops and his mind freezes and then it slowly thaws.

"Yeh, seriously. Could be the most important thing you ever do."

Guy looks over at me, quizzical. I mean, he does deals every day, seven eight figures, whaddaya mean 'most important'?

"No but I mean like: *really* married. Till death you depart. Not like some guys, they contract a marriage like they check into a whorehouse. Then dump the bitch and on you go. No I mean like, a *real* marriage. Dig? Where you're like ... faithful ... not because you *gotta* be ... but because you *can* be ... cause it's a way of giving thanks.

"And that departin' death stuff — you take that serious! Cause I mean like — here's hoping you both get old together, and dandle your grandchildren, and you die very quietly with a final prayer. But maybe you don't — maybe you die a day later — hot lead ripping through your heart and arteries, soon there's nothin' left a you but a chalk outline ona sidewalk and some yellow tape. But you left her a seed ... and it grows, and it — OH, man ... !" and Murphy's losing it, head down on the table just losing it,

"Don't do it man, don't go there,

don't do it less you really mean it man, I mean you got no idea,

you got like — no idea at all, what a big deal this is. It's like — it's like dyin' but it's like — it's more like, like bein' born."

HOT ROCKS

So it's a normal day, and we're sitting around. Joey's got his feet up, reading a mystery magazine.

"Whadaya read that trash for, Joey, it's all just made up. Now *this*, this is the ticket," and I show him one of my true-detective kinds. "See, all real cases. The genuine article. Like lookit this one. Guy ties her up, slashes her nude on a waterbed, then makes soup with her bones, *with* the water in the waterbed. Really happened. Y'oughta read this stuff, learn a lot about real life."

Joey sighs. "Well, maybe, Murphy," he says, leaning back and with this summer-soft look behind his eyes. "But me I like it where the P.I., he's solving all these murders and getting shot at and getting kissed by broads and hoofing it down the mean streets and telling the Mob to back off and the D.A. to take a walk ... 'cos it's all so sweet, so just sweet, you could almost really believe, even although you never really see it, not in real life. Anyhow not our real life."

My jaw sags. "Aw, Joey, you got me depressed again."

He sits up straight. "Only one thing for that."
"Pizza!"
"With onions!"
"And anchovies!"
"You're on!"

So we pool the contents of our pockets and Joey heads off for La Mama's — best 'za in town, but a ways away. On foot, 'cos the car we been using, what we found, been repo'd, maybe by the rightful owner.

So me I go back to reading about this true case, the Kannibal Killer they called him, finally got caught by the entrails on his breath. But as for me, no case, no action, and after a while I drop the magazine.

So I'm back on my ownsome, just me, just plain old Murphy, gazing out the window to pass the time, wondering if anything might someday happen; when before you know it there are footsteps outside the door. I perk up. They stop. I stay perked. They pick up again: and then: In walks this palooka, pale as ice.

He stops, his eyes barely flicker at me and he slowly rotates his gaze, scanning the room, just taking me in with the rest of the mess. He's got his hair shaved short, the color of toothbrush bristles. Ice-cream suit with neat creases. Rings on more fingers than one.

"Jee-*zuss* what a dump." He looks around, shaking his head. I look around too. Then he shrugs; the whole thing is beyond him. "Well, so much the better, for the matter of that. Take a guy a month in this mess to find even something that *wasn't* hidden. — So look, pal, I got a job for you, you dumb-lucky second-rate shamus. You earn five hunner bucks for doin' nothin'."

"Sounds great. Fork over the five hunnert an' get the hell out."

"Nn-O-ho, not *that* kinda nothin'. I leave something here for safe-keeping, I come back ... well, when things quiet down, could be a week, might be a month." He dangles a little violet velvet bag.

I stare at it. It's going back and forth, back and forth. "What's in there?"

He frowns, then shrugs. "What the heck, you'll peek anyway." With a touch of modest pride. "*Di'mints*." And he keeps dangling and dangling the bag.

"Hm." I consider this. A thought occurs to me. "Stolen?"

"What the *hell* do you think?" He gives me a disgusted look, then glances again at the room, as if for confirmation.

But I give him one right back. "Don't bother me. Blow."

"Say what?" He pretends to be deaf.

"Scram. Beat it. Fade. This ain't a locker, I ain't innarested in your rocks."

He looks at me with eyes like eggs over easy, walks around me full circle, looking me up and down. "I don't believe this. I have seen dumb, but this man is *dumb*. Five hunner big ones, yours for the taking. Candy from a baby, fruit on the vine. Whassa matter wichoo, you don't know the value of money?"

"I know the value of — ah, the heck wit'it, you woulden even know the word."

He nods, quick, like a jack-in-the-box. "Yeh, it figures. Guy lives in a dive like this, crud all over the

145

walls, crap in the alleys, furniture is crates and rejects from the Salvation Army."

I sigh; I don't dispute this. Rejects from the Salvation Army is about right.

He goes on with a tight grin. "It figures a guy like that has got himself right where he belongs. You wouldn't know a dime from a donut. So long, moron. I ain't got time."

He blows out the door and I pick up my magazine.

Time passes, taking its time doing it. I look at my wrist where a watch would go. I look at the calendar — babe in a swimsuit, grinning as she wields a power saw; it hasn't changed. Plenty of time to turn over golden memories in the mind, if only I could remember.

And then more clumping up the stairs, and with no knock or Simon-Says-May-I, this dark-haired guy to see me, hey the Murphy social calendar is really sizzling today. This one's short, but muscled, and his eyebrows are like two thumb-smudges. He grins, which is not an improvement, as most of the teeth are just holes, and the rest are black with tobacco.

" 'ce place ya got here," he says, checking it out.

I shrug. Everyone's a critic.

He scans through the open doorway to the back room. "And you here all by your lonesome."

"Hey, the dog pound's two doors down, so take a hike. I'm busy."

"You don't *look* bu-sy ..."

"I'm doin' my nails."

He nods, not like he heard me, and circles slowly around the room. He takes in the comic-book stacks, the piles of pizza boxes, the broken things and the things I was gonna fix up, other things set aside for sorting later; he toes aside a garbage bag, peers under it, loses interest, gets a faraway look. He pauses before the moose head in the sink, and murmurs polite appreciation. He peeks into the half-open drawers full of hardware and underwear. He nods again. "No wonder he picked this dump. A great place to stash something. A museum, a maze."

"Yeh well, the maid died and she couldn't come in. Now breeze, I'm expecting company."

He grinned again. Made him look like a rat in heat for some cheese.

"You already had your company, smart guy. Whitey. I shadowed him here and waited till he came out. Then I caught up with him on Blate Street and tossed him: and he was clean. So it stands to reason. A haul like that doesn't just vanish into thin air. Where's the ice?"

"Whadaya — Outa here — I don't have ..."

I stopped. I was going to tell him I don't have it, and he can believe me or not; but then I figure, what's it his business? I don't even like this guy. "I don't — have — to talk to you."

He smiles like an egg frying at the edges. "You sure don't, lone little guy like me." He whistles, and whomp, a hulk lumbers in, with a grin and a gun. "But you do gotta talk to *us*."

I leap for the doorway but the big guy just plays door. The ratty guy grabs me and I jab him, then the big guy pins my arms back and the other guy slips me on some cuffs. They seat me down, then the big guy goes off and fishes out a comic book and sits down to study it while the hard guy stands over me, hands on hips, looking down.

I consider the situation, informally tot up the pros and cons — from where I'm sitting, mostly cons — but then somehow lose interest, and just sit there.

"All right, you know what I want. Sing!"

"Um ... Could you hum a few bars?"

"Oh, a wise guy! — But that's okay, I like wise guys. So wise up before I smack you across your wise-guy mouth."

Oh great, I think, trying not to be bored, two wise guys in a room, one in handcuffs, one with a sap.

"And just to help you out, yeh, I'll sing a few bars."

He puts his face very close to mine, which I really wish he didn't, and to the tune, give or take, of "Good King Whatsisface," he begins to rasp out:

"*If* I wish to keep my balls,
I will spill the bee-heans!
I will tell this nice man all,
I will come quite clea-hean!"

"Hm yeh," I mumble. "Nice song. Rings a bell."

"W-*with*-th-th ..."

Uh-oh, a refrain. He brandishes his sap. "Old MacDonald" this time — really a medley of old favorites.

" ... a *bop bop* here, an' a
whap whap there —
here a *bop*, there a *bop* — "

 ... and the whole time he's fitting the deed to the word.

Gotta admit, it does help you keep time to the beat. My head's sagging, still not saying anything, 'cos what's to say? I got nothing to say to this guy. I don't want to know him better; don't want to be his friend; and if I'm in need of a light, I'll ask someone else. I'm not enjoying this, it's not what you'd choose, given the choice — which, note, I was not; but before, I was bored, and now I'm not bored.

He's whacking me and chatting.

"You know, them jogger jerks is got it all wrong. Best exercise ya can get is beating guys up. It uses the fist muscles, the wrist muscles, uses the arm muscles, shoulder muscles; uses the knee muscles," he adds, demonstrating to my midriff, "even the elbow and" *whomp* "head muscles. Keeps *me* in shape, bends *you* out of it."

So he keeps it up a bit and then *he* gets bored, or disappointed, or maybe he just lost his train of thought. He scratches his head and shrugs and goes to the fridge, peers in and is pleasantly surprised. "My brand!" he says, admiringly; and reaches out a Mickey's. He asks do I want one and I shake my head no. He asks do I got any pretzels, and it's hard to talk, what with the swelling and the blood, but with a quick sideways nod I indicate over in the corner, behind the chair. So he sips and munches and thinks and crunches — other guy still on his comic book the whole while — then he gets an idea. He goes and carefully undoes my belt, me watching this with interest; tugs down the trousers, and lowers the drawers. Me I do nothing. Still your move.

He takes out a Zippo, crouches down, and flicks it. "Hate to do this, pal, but you're wasting my time."

Now I'm not liking this. Two thumbs down. Right now I'd rather be bored.

He flicks it again, and another time, but no flame. Damn thing's out of fluid, flint's shot, whatever. He curses and throws it away. "You got any matches?"

"Yeah, up in the — No but I mean, *sheesh!*" What a nerve. I mean, the guy's a guest and all, but still, there's limits.

So he's slapping his pockets, no go, doesn't smoke, that's good, bad habit; then he's rummaging around in the rubble in the sink, knocking things about, starting to curse — bad habit, that. He flings open a cupboard and some stuff falls out and he's pawing around in that and all this time the bigger guy doesn't lift a finger to help, doesn't seem to know what's going on, just concentrating on his comic, moving his lips, having trouble with some of the words. The rat guy is thrashing, tossing things this way and that, sweating and swearing; and meanwhile I'm musing: if I can just stall him a little longer, Joey should be back. He'd have been back by now already if we'd phoned in our order first, only, little disagreement with the phone company about a bill, so no phone, he's got to go wait while they bake it.

Suddenly he shouts out, "Aha! I found your stash."

What, which stash? Not those embarrassing — oh, the match stash. *Zhit.* That stash.

He's chuckling, back in humor. "He-hey, I got quite a choice here," fingering the various matchbooks. 'Ben's Bowling Lanes; 'Big Bob's Beef Barn'; 'The Oasis — Fine Booze and Drink.' Oh and here's a novelty item: 'What did the nun say to the stockbroker?' and then it tells you inside. Ha! Pretty funny. 'Dirk's Diner', 'Ed's Eats', 'Ollie's Oyster Bar'." He looks up. "What, you collect these? 'Can U Draw This? U May Have Talent', and then they show ... heck, it's just a circle! What is this, an audition or a sobriety test? Oh and here's one: 'Earn Big $$$ in your Spare Time. Become a Famous Private Eye. Details Inside'. — Hey, looks like you shoulda sent away for that one!"

I'm gnawing my lip and not laughing at his jokes. He likes it I laugh at his jokes. But no dice. Even if they're funny. Principle of the thing.

"All right, tough guy. This'll loosen up your jaw." He lights a match, holds it and gazes at it, twin flames dancing, dancing, dancing in his eyes.

"Awright, I *tellya!*" Little sweat jobs popping out on my brow.

He smiles and waves out the match. "So tell me."

My face is wet and my mouth is dry. "It's — it's under a floorboard."

"Ah! An excellent choice. And, which floorboard, if you don't mind my inquiring?"

My hands are bound but I point to it with a little jerk of the head. "Right there, right under the radiator."

He grins. "Now you're talking. Y'know, you're a good conversationalist when you loosen up a little." He walks over, bends down, then stands up scowling. "There's like half an inch of clearance! How the heck am I supposed to pry that thing up."

I lick my lip, though the tongue is dry. "You just gotta move the radiator, is all."

"I just gotta move the radiator." He is staring at me like I am insane.

"Right. You got it. Just — budge it a bit. No big deal."

He nudges it with his foot, uncertainly; no go. "The damned thing's bolted to the floor!" He starts to reach for the matches.

"Relax relax. I got tools."

"You got — you got move-the-radiator tools."

"Right. Exactly. It's like a kit. Everything you ever needed for moving your radiator around. Got it at the hardware."

"So where is this kit."

"Well, it got kinda scattered. There's a screwdriver up in that top cupboard, shelf way at the back ..."

He's standing on tip-toes and rummaging and tugging, things falling all over him, pulling other things out and then those things come pulling *other* things out, when all at once the whole cupboard comes crashing down. I kept meaning to fix that. "What th — "

"No it's okay, it's okay. You got it. And there's a pliers right under the sink, way in back, behind the pipes ..." and time is ticking and he hasn't even found the screwdriver yet, he's banging around and yanking things down, really making a mess, really; when suddenly he wises up.

"He-ey, wait a minute."

"I'll wait. A minute, two minutes. Whatever you say. I got all day."

"Wait a — *wait* a minute. Whitey was only in here for like what, a few minutes tops, the guy with the ice, then he left and he ran and we caught up with him and we come straight here. You only had like ten minutes at the outside, how'd you have time to move out the radiator and mess with the floorboard and stow the stash and fix the radiator back and clean up and all that? You're tugging my nuts!"

"Spoken like a detective. Only, maybe I didn't and maybe I did, but the fact is: You'll never know what is under that floorboard, unless you look."

Wild, he stares over at it. Tick, tick, hurry, Joey.

"You'll lie awake nights, years later, thinking: Damn, I coulda had it all! The guy mighta been telling the truth, *why didn't I look?* Diamonds, bright diamonds, beyond the dreams of avarice! Diamonds, there for the taking! You'd'a been the Emperor of Easy Street, 'stead of scrounging your dinner in the gutter, 'stead of dying off jacking off in some SRO, since the homeless shelter wouldn't even let you in. Dying like a dog, when you coulda had it all. You'll hate yourself and want to end it all, but all you can find is a spoon, and—"

"Shaddup," he says, his hand in my face like a half-grapefruit. "Bruto, give me a hand with this. Or a foot." So Bruto lumbers up and goes over and kicks over the radiator and stomps on the floorboard which it was loose anyway and up it pops and he goes back and sits down with his comic book and the rat man peers down into the hole but no dice. No ice.

He looks over at me now like I'm not his best buddy anymore. "You lied to me."

"Gee that's funny I was sure it was there."

"You *lied* to me!"

"I did. That was wrong of me. Very wrong."

"*Liar*!!"

"Alright keep your shirt on. I'll remember next time I go to Confession."

"Confession time *now*, pal." He goes for the match pile.

Hurry, Joey.

"Which do you figure burns brightest, pal? 'Biff's Bar'? 'Jim's Gym'? 'Call Cathy 4 a Good Time'?"

C'mon Joey, pizza's getting cold. Don't stop to admire the flowers, the little plastic guys in a circle around the dead sapling where the dogs poop. Don't stop to chat with deaf old Mrs. Carrera. Hurry home while it's hot. And before I am.

"He-ey," holding it up. "This should be a good one. *Repent, or Taste the Licking Fires of Hell.* Match-jacket all in crimson. And then a number to call."

He carefully selects a match and strikes it, holding it for a moment to make sure the flame has caught. "*I'm* your number, now, chum." He kneels down. "Time to get on the call-in hotline and talk."

Now I'm not liking this at all. Sucks, really. And yet my mind is somewhere else. On Joey, and on … other stuff.

The wavering flame casts highlights over the rat man's glistening face.

And then — and then, there he is, my brother, coming in whistling; but then his whistle dies. He stands in the doorway, holding aloft the pizza, looking around, taking in the scene.

Now like — *you*. What do *you* do. You come home, coupla plug-ugglies got your best brother shackled and spread-eagled and they're about to fry his manhood. What do you do — drop the pizza? An X-tra Large, fresh from the oven, with everything, with more than everything, with extra anchovies and with extra hot-peppers in a little plastic dish to the side, splashing all over the floor?

Not Joey. He goes over to the counter, clears a space with the edge of the box and sets it down carefully. The two guys are not moving, only following with their eyes. Nobody saying anything and the match burns down and singes the rat man's fingers and he drops it and stifles a curse. Then Joey moves over towards us.

The two guys are still pretty cool 'cos like, they got gats and he doesn't; plus the bigger guy has dropped his comic and now he's standing right next to the rat-man, shoulder to shoulder, blocking the path to myself, who am watching all this with renewed interest. The rat man says, just a skosh bit nervous now as Joey slowly comes on, "Now just, you just keep out of this, hear. Doesn't concern you. Plus something in it for you, you play it cool. Heck yes, split it three ways."

"My brother you got there," observes Joey, with a nod in my direction to make his meaning clear.

The hard guys exchange a quick look, then back at Joey; and a sneer of complete contempt comes into view, as the rat man raises his gat and relaxes. "What's yer problem, big guy. Are you your brother's keeper?"

And Joey roars: "You bet your fuckin' ass I am!"

He lunges, he's like insane. Bullets wing him, he just comes on. He grabs the two of them by the ears and clonks their heads together, clonks 'em again, and it's like ... I don't really wanna describe it. It's like, you ever bought a sack of tomatoes, then somebody sat on 'em, and somebody shat on 'em? Like that. Joey's raging, he's like this animal, this beautiful animal, go Joey go, and I'm lovin' my brother, I love that solid son of a —

It's all over.

He wipes his brow and tries to smile. then rifles the guy's pockets and fishes out the key to the cuffs He springs me and I rub my wrists.

"Whachoo been up to, Murphy?"

"Just workin' up an appetite."

"I got the stuff for that, Murphy. And would you believe it — they was havin' a special." He serves up the pie, pulls a six-pack out of the fridge.

We pull a couple of crates up to the table, and Joey cocks his head over his shoulder while we chow down. "Who're those guys, Murph?"

I point to my mouth, finish the mouthful, then say: "Couple dead bozos, used to be live wires."

On his mighty forehead, a tiny frown. "You figure we oughta call the cops?"

I shake my head — mouth full again.

"What — call the garbage collection?"

"Hey, first things first, and last things later. Serve me up another slice of that stuff."

He forks me a wide one.

"Mm-mm, man! That was worth waiting for."

"Pass the salt, brother. They never makes these things salty enough."

So we're musing and munching, and then I say, "Took you a while. Getting worried there."

He remembers something. "I almost forgot! Thing that held me up a bit — there's this." And he pulls out the little violet velvet bag!

I stare at it. Sure enough, the same one.

"Know what's in there?"

"No, I ain't looked."

"It's worse than dirt. No good can come of it. Just throw it out."

He shrugs, and dumps it in the trash.

"So whereja get it?"

"Craziest thing. I'm walkin' to the 'ria and this albino guy comes tearing down the sidewalk, lickety split, followed by a big guy and a little guy — He-ey, could even of been these guys. Anyhow, he's just rounded the corner, and he stuffs the bag in my mug and says, "*take it!*", really hot and hoarse. And I figure, it's something the two palookas wanna take offen 'im. So like, he's probly gonna lose it either way, y'know? But, like, me, in his shoes, I'd of faked and switchbacked and balled the jack and hightailed it, at least have a chance; plus when they caught up with him later and he didn't have it, they might of got sore. But him, he pushes it onto me, losing it for sure, and maybe coming in for a beating, just so those two won't get it. Just like to say, *Fuck you* to those two. I mean, that make sense to you?"

"Sure," I say, rubbing my chin. "Fact of the matter, it makes perfect sense to me."

~ *The End* ~

MURPHY IN A MOOD OF ATTRITION

Why do I do these things? Why do I do these things?
It's crazy — Sometimes I don't even enjoy them.
 ...
 ... ... only ... fact a the matter,
most of the time I **do** enjoy them.
Just plain straight fact: I like it a lot.
So maybe I'll have to log an extra 50,000 laps in
Purgatory,
for what I done, last night alone.
I can handle it. Heck, a hangover can be just as bad.
So when I do something crazy, I'll *try* to repent;
but if I *can't* repent, there's no such thing as faking it.
I just say to St. Peter, "Put it on my tab."

HELLO YOURSELF

It was fiscal Friday, and the Murphy brothers, up for anything but down on their luck, were taking stock.

"How we doin', Joey?"

"Not so good, Murphy." He stared into the drawer and shook his head. "We got a half a pack a Camels, a trading stamp, a wooden nickel, some matchbooks that one of 'em is practally new, got a subway token only wrong city, and a couple of coupons from before the war."

"Not so good." I sighed. "Looks like we gotta dig into our strategic reserves, Joey." It had come to this. "Bring out the empties."

And then my brother looked shamefaced.

"Had to hock 'em, Murphy."

My eyes went out on stalks. "You *pawned* our *empties*, Joey?"

"Had to, Murphy."

"You don't — *pawn* ... **empties**, Joey."

"All we had left, Murphy."

I held my head hard, sorta press the thoughts together. "Oo-ooh, uh-ohhhh, — okay. Now I gotta think of *another* clever plan, so's we can get some scratch, s'we can get our empties outa hock, s'we can trade 'em in and make a killing and go get lunch. Looks like a long morning, Joey. Gotta think, concentrate. Bring me a beer."

He looked at me sadly.

"We — we're all out, Murphy." I stared at him. He was biting his lip.

"Ahh, hey — heck, d'worry about it. 'm not thirsty anyway. Only ... You reckon we get a pizza on credit?"

"Not any more, Murphy. That well's dry."

So that was it, then. The old old story. The old wolf at the old door. Had to go hustle up a buck, somehow — but for a P.I., it's not that easy to drum up business. Just calling up folks on the phone and ask do they need a detective, sir or madam, is not how it's done. Though the average guy, he'd stop to think of it, there's a lot of things he might want to use me for.

I grabbed yesterday's paper, freshest we had, and — well first I re-read the comic strips, I mean some of them are just a scream — but then I hunkered down and scanned the personals and the want ads. "Rodney, Darling, do come home. Mother's gone and all is forgiven." Hey, just my meat, a missing person; only by the sound of it he'd come back all by himself, wagging his little tail behind him. — Clean-up crew needed at the local j.c. Hmm, *might* be my line, maybe a body was found in the library. — "Sober individual of cleanly habits not afraid of hard work needed for — " Nope. — Here's one: "Pizza taster needed for major supplier. Name your own salary. Free beer." I blinked, and it turned back into an ad for a suspensory salesman. "Jeez, I'm so parched, I'm startin'a see a mirage."

Joey meanwhile had got an idea of his own. Out under our big sign that says "MURPHY BROS. — PRIVATE INVESTIGATORS," he had tacked up a paper one he wrote out with crayon, saying: "SPECIAL TODAY." He stood back; nodded; smiled.

So we wait. And we fast like it's Lent. Who knows, maybe even slip in a prayer here and there. And before you know it, there's a swish — swish — swish on the stairs, and both of us are sitting up straight.

Just like in the picture show. A dame walks in, a class dame. Heels up on stilts, blood-red nails, rings 'n' things. A slinky dress, one a them tube jobs, that hits her curves in overdrive. Standard-issue lip, curled back from the pearly-whites in a kind of sneer. My kind of dame.

"You're probably wondrin' why I come here 'stead of some class joint," she says, looking bored.

"Um, yeh. Matter fact, same idea was jumpin' through my mind."

"Fact is, I need somebody tough."

"You're lookin' at 'im."

"Rough."

"Rough? We got rough, got it in spades." I go into my stance and poke a couple of jabs into the air.

"Somebody ... not afraid to bend a few rules."

"Rules, what's that? Never heard of 'em. I'll bend anybody, lady, fork over the dough."

"Cos you see," she went on, kind of a grim smile, "some classy guy what's up and coming, got a upscale business to protect, he might not want to risk his license if the going gets rough. But you — you got nothing to lose."

While I'm biting my tongue and steaming at this, Joey puts in: "A course, it's gotta be legit. Gotta be all on the up 'n' up."

Her head turns on its neck like a periscope and she blinks at him like he took a wrong turn back at Mars. I rush in with "Yeh, right. Um, yagotta, yagotta tell us on your honor, lady, that it's on the up 'n' up."

Her eyes go to the one, then to the other of us, but like not seeing. "On my — ? ... ! ... You guys are rich."

"That we ain't not, lady, but we got our, our standards, like. Only since you bring it up, we could actually just at present use a piece or two of spare change."

"I see. And what are your, ah, rates."

"Rates. Right. Our rates. We got those, Joey? Lemme see. Whata we say — Twenny bucks a day plus expenses. In cash. Up front. No coupons, no bounced checks."

She sort of snorts. "That's ... very reasonable. Only how about you ballpark these 'expenses'."

"Well, lessee. Gotta consult with my associate. What's a Large goin' for at Mama Rosa's these days, Joey?"

"What, with everything?"

"Course with everything!"

"Setcha back fifteen big ones, Murphy."

"Okay so, expenses, you 'n' me, fifteen 'n' fifteen, that's thirty right there. Making fifty, all told. Figure you can swing it?"

"I can swing it."

"Okay great, so we're in business. So what's the job."

Her eyes got thin and business-like. "I wancha you catch a rat."

"Rat, eh. A bad apple?"

"One a the worst."

"What 'e do ta ya?"

"I wouldn't wanna say it in mix company. But after that he made off with six grand in C notes I'd been saving for a slimy day."

"Hm, that's bad. Grand larceny, absconding — bad, very bad. — Okay, we'll check it out, and if it checks out, we'll get you back your six grand."

Again the ruby-red slid back from the sharp whites. "The grands I can handle. What you do is, you find him for me, you tell me *where* he's gonna be, *when*."

That old sinking feeling. "Uhh, lady ..."

She flicked on the charm switch. "Call me Stella."

"Yeh so okay, uh, Stella: look. We may be hungry but we're not just from hunger. We don't do repo, don't do divorce work, and we sure as heck don't set up hits."

She put her hand with all the rings over her décolleté and her long thin fingers bent back. "No-ho, boys, hey, you got me all wrong. The green stuff you're just helping walk back to its rightful owner, and as for him, he's loaded, won't even miss it. For divorce, forget it, we're not even married, we were just livinagether, is all. And as for that other thing, no, it's just, I just wanna say hi, is all, and chew the fat with him. Sure! He gives me what's mine, all is forgiven. Sure! Maybe even move back in together — sure!"

"And maybe make it legal?" Joey puts in hopefully.

Her head is back, laughing, red throat and white teeth. "Sure, go legitimate, why not!"

"*Honest*?" says Joey, his eyes in earnest. "You really mean it?"

"I give you my word of — what you said."

I'm shaking my head and I'm pacing around. I don't like it, but you know what beggars can't be. And it *might* be okay, if we work it right. I mean you never can tell; it *might* be ...

"O-kay," I said wearily, "so give us the scoop. And our daily."

She flicked open a silver pocketbook shaped like the wedge of an ax, fished out a fifty from a slim leather wallet, fished around some more and came up with a photograph. I snuck a peek into the pocketbook — lots of practice from looking down dress fronts — and spotted a tiny pearl-handled revolver, with a death's-head carved in the pearl.

"Nice lookin' guy," said Joey, flicking the snapshot with a fingernail.

"He's alright," she shrugged. "Name's Jim Ranger. Case he's disguised himself any, he's got a tattoo of a serpent on his left arm, and a mole right on his ... well, never mind about the mole. Talks with a drawl, hangs out in pool-halls. But he's lyin' low, 'cos my boys — 'cos I just can't find him."

"Hm, pool halls, huh?" said Joey. "I like a man plays pool. You know we got our own table, right ina back room? So what place does he like special? Maybe we find him there."

"Oh, who knows," she said, irritably. "Low-class dives, joints with no class to 'em. Can't remember their names."

"Hmm." Joey got thoughtful. "Now there's Crambo's, that's pretty funky. Great tables. And Jomo's — a real dump. And Barotti's — now that's a great place — low as you can go!"

She looked at him sort of startled. "Say, Barotti's, that sounds right, actually. Knew it had a wop name."

"We'll get right on it," I said. "Meantime, where do we reach you."

"You don't. Like my privacy. But I'll contact you, here or wherever you can be reached, at noon and at seven every day."

She starts for the door and Joey pockets the photo, whistling, but me an evil tune is running through my mind. "Just a second!" I say, and she stops. "That twenty and expenses was just for our time, win or lose.

But we find him, it's a bonus five hundred on top a that."

She didn't bat a false eyelash. "Sure."

When she was good and gone, I said: "Joey, we got a problem."

He looked at me leery. "You think she's a wrong dame?"

"Put it this way, Joey. I don't care how she got the six grand in the first place, and for all I know this Jimbo made off with it. For all me, she can have it back. But what bothers me is what she aims to do with him. This all-is-forgiven business, I just don't know about that. Maybe, maybe not. We just got to play our cards careful, is all. Find out if he took it, shake him up if necessary, get the bread and even steven, he can walk away from there."

"She told us on her honor — "

"Problem is, Joey, her honor and a dollar you can ride the bus."

That glummed him down some. "Not fair, Murphy. I wanna work for the good guys."

"Yeh well, me too, only right now she's the best we got. So do your best."

We xeroxed the photo at the corner drug and then split up. Joey for Crambo's, me for Barotti's. Not likely we'd find a hair of him, but maybe we'd find someone who knew someone, who for a suitable compensation might tell us where Ranger had taken off to.

Downstairs at Barotti's, the way they got it set up is, the bar's the first thing you see as you go in. And this was good, because I needed a beer to cool down and think things over. The bartender brought me a tall one without I even ask, like the way you get a glass of water at Schrafft's.

So I thought, and I thought some more, and the more I thought, the less I liked what I was thinking. There was something about that frail that spelled bad news. Just a kind of a feeling — call it P.I. intuition. The color of her money was right and right welcome, but she had the same damn color in her eyes.

Still, a man's gotta make a living. But what a life!

It was early yet, the place was just beginning to fill up. A joint like this, it's always early until it's too late.

I craned my neck and licked away the foam and looked around me, wondering which one of these citizens might have a line on our man. Wouldn't do to be too direct about it, might scare them off. Way it's done is — first you drink awhile, spend some, then you chat a bit, just a offhand comment here and there, set up your creds; then it turns out you and some other guy root for the same team, what a fantastic coincidence, I mean what are the chances of that; and like that; and finally you buy him a beer. Then you toss out a question here, a query there, maybe hint at something; and if nothing comes of it, at least you're drunk. That's how the professionals operate; with me, it's second nature. So I'm scanning the place, sipping slowly, peering out over the top of the glass, getting ready to make my move.

Just then a sandy-haired fellow ambles over to the bar, says something makes me choke on my suds. "Hey, anybody seen Jim Ranger?"

I turn around and I give him the gaping gray eyeball. I stand up. "'S funny you should mention that," I say, "cos I'm looking for a fella goes by that handle. Tall guy, with a drawl?"

"Yeh, that's Jim all right. He's a regular."

I drained my glass to hide my expression, head-wheels turning furiously. What was that damn dame's game, and who was doing the scoring? All of this was happening much too fast.

By now, all eyes were on me. Faces like in poker, pony up you wanna see these cards. I eyed them back, didn't like what I was seeing. More guys filtering in, looking me coolly up and down. I shrugged and backed off.

"Ahh, only I heard, what I heard is, the guy is laying low, so this must be a different guy."

"Laying low, Jim? Not the Jim I know. He just been out of town is all. Got back last night I heard."

"Oh. Ahh, so this Jim you know," the eyes get shrewd, "does he have a snake tattoo on his left — on his right arm?"

The fellow frowned his sandy eyebrows, then cocked his head at the bartender, who shrugged. He turned back to me. "I don't know. I never noticed."

"Oh well then, a thing like that, you'd notice; must be a different guy. Thanks anyway." I slid off the barstool. "I'll just be heading along ..."

"Upper arm or lower?" asked Sandy.

"Oh, I — oh. I don't know."

"Cos it was upper, you wouldn't see it. Dresses nice, Jim does. Not like some people." He frowns at me. "Not the kind of guy rolls a pack a Camels up in his tee-shirt sleeve."

"Mm, yeh, sure. Still, pretty common name, Jim is; plus I reckon everybody's named Ranger that his daddy was. Probably just a coincidence."

"Sa-ay ... Isn't that a picture of Jim's head you got pokin' out a your pocket?"

I looked down. The snapshot. "What, this?" Stalling for time.

"Yeh, that." He plucked it out and nodded. "That's Jim all right."

I grabbed it back and stuffed it in my trousers. "No well see, that, it's a bad likeness. The light and everything. So I'll just — "

"Hey!" said Sandy, looking up and waving. "There's Jim now!"

A tall friendly-faced fellow that by now I'd know him anywhere walked in slapping palms and socking shoulders all around. Someone called out from the back, "How was Cleveland?" and he smiled and called back "Could be worse. But not much." Then he hoisted himself up onto the free stool beside me, and announced to all concerned that actually things had gone pretty well, so far as his-truly, and he called for beers all round. I got one too, though he didn't know me.

And as I watched him laughing and joking and drinking, unaware of what was maybe in store for him, I decided that I'd go through with it, but that I'd play it absolutely straight with him. If he'd had sticky fingers they would have to come unstuck, but there was no way I was going to set him up for a hit.

When we'd both drained our glasses I said to him low, out of the side of my mouth: "Stella sent me to find you."

A kind of haze came over his eyes and his mouth seemed not to know what to do and it showed just the leftover traces of a smile. Then he slid an arm round my shoulder and we got off our stools and went over to an empty booth off to the side.

"So how is she," he said; and he stuck a smoke in his face to give it something to do.

"Could be better," I said, "though I've seen worse."

A sort of rueful smile. "Yeah, that's Stella. So what's she up to these days."

Now normally I'd say, "Oh, you know, just the usual things," working my game; only like I said, I'd decided to play it straight.

"That's just what I'm not sure of." I leaned forward. "Look, I'll lay it out for you. She sent me to get back six yards she says you swiped from her. You got it?"

He considered me coolly, blowing smoke in twin jets from his nose. "I got it. Still got the original bills, original wrappers. Only, swiped it or not, maybe I see it a different way."

"All right. Listen. Hand over the six G's and we'll call it even. Why she thinks you might give it back, just like that, I don't know, but if I have to find out, I'll do it. I'd rather just keep this whole thing from getting ugly for everyone."

He nodded. "Go on."

"And the other thing is, — she wants me to finger you. And that I'm not willing to do."

He did kind of a one-eyebrow frown and stubbed his butt, then lit another one, squinting up his eyes. Then he cocked one of them at me as he shook out the match. "Finger me? For what?"

I had nothing in the hole so I laid out the cards. "What she *claims* is, she just wants to see you, say hi. Bury the old hatchet and talk over old times. Only what I'm not sure is whose head she means to bury the hatchet *in*."

He looked at me real, real carefully. "So you're working for Stella. So why are you telling me all this."

I sighed, next door to dejected. "Look, Jim — I call you Jim? — I'm not going to lead a man into something that it might be a trap, unless he done a heck of a lot more than what you did, so far as I know so far. Now you're a generous guy, you bought the beers, so why not just buy this dame off. Maybe you see the incident different, but she sees it her way, and from where she's sitting she got ripped off, and who's to say where the truth lies? Most guys give themselves the benefit of every doubt. So surprise yourself and give her the benefit of this one; I reckon *I* did or I wouldn't even be here. Plus if she's really just all wet and there's no doubt at all, still, I figure it's worth the six grand to you to know that she's out there gunning for you."

He was nodding as I said my piece, staring at the tabletop, and when he looked up again he had that kind of philosophical look around the eyes you get after a change of heart or a few beers. "You know, you're all right, Mister — "

"Murphy. Call me Murphy."

"You're all right, and what's more, you may be right. I maybe been too hard on old Stella." He raised his chin over at the barkeep and signaled for a pitcher. "You say she wants to see me?"

"Yeh, but — what she wants is I tell her where you'll be at a certain time. Like she'd like to surprise you. Says her. And in this business — "

"You know, that's sweet of her. A surprise! I musta misjudged her. I mean, she has her faults, we all know that, but it takes all kinds. I mean, to think that she should make the first move!"

"But — "

"Tell you what. What say I come around to your office. I bring the cash, you bring Stella, and we find out what bygones can be."

When I hooked up with Joey, he was looking pretty mellow. "No go at Crambo's, come up empty; did shoot some pool, though, won a coupla bucks. You?"

And I told him about the big break in the case.

We fixed it up he'd drop by about twelve thirty, but he showed up early and Joey took him into the back room to shoot pool. His old old-lady called in at the dot of noon. I told her to hurry over; "We got a break in the case."

Ten minutes later she turns up on our doorstep. She's breathing heavily. "You got a lead?"

"We found him."

"Ha! Can you believe it." She snatched the telephone on my desk without even asking, and dialed. "Hello, Rico? Find the Smiler — he can't have gone far. Be ready to move. Call you back in five."

I was indignant. "First of all, that'll be ten cents, lady, for the phone call. Plus what, it sounds like you were setting up a hit!"

She tossed her raven locks at me contemptuously. "What if I was."

That really steamed me, and I practically screamed at her. "So that's just it, huh, that's it, huh, just like that. You think I'm a crud, a moral moron, just stand here while you set it up and don't even try to hide it, go ahead, you can say whatever you like in front of the servants, they don't exist. So like I'm just gonna stand here and stand for it, is that it?"

She shrugged. "Why not? You're in it this far already."

"Well I'm not having any! You can whistle for it, bitch! I'm not telling you where he is."

She started to snap open her handbag. "So you stumbled on some scruples. It's too late for that."

Just then the door from the back room opened, revealing Jim Ranger, tall and calm as he could be; and what he held in his hand was no rinkydoodle pearl handled plaything like she was fishing around for. It was a .44 magnum; no frills, just kills.

"Hello Stella." He stood; he said.

Her eyes got wild, she looked back and forth between us. But when she spoke, it was to me. "You brought him *here*? You — *idiot*." And the acid in her eyes could melt steel.

"She's right, you know, Murphy old sport," Jim said, not taking his eyes off her but in a conversational tone. "It is too late." And then to her: "So, you're using the Smiler? Low." Sad shake of the head. "The guy's got no loyalty. Have to have a chat with him about that."

Then just then Joey comes in, buttoning up from the john. He stares in horror at the scene, and stops still.

Jim goes on, his voice getting tighter, but not louder.

"So: You thought you ought to keep the gee's you lifted off that sugar-daddy you were stepping out with on the sly. Well, we could argue that; but I won't waste words." The gun lifted almost imperceptibly — but we perceived, we perceived. "*This* is for two-timing me — " and he blasts apart her gun-hand as it scrambles around frantically in her handbag. " — and *this* is for trying to have me killed." A shot to the midriff and she goes down in a pile.

He stood over her prostrate body, already twitching with the last of life. "And *this* ... *this* ... is for your lowdown ways."

He aims for her lying tongue and her head explodes in a million pieces. The smoke rolls away and is gone.

He pockets the rod and smiles at us. "I'd say sorry about the carpet, if you had one." Joey's looking like he's going to be sick and is biting his fist.

"I been wondering what to do about you two," he went on casually. "Normally ... But you been straight with me, and the fact is, you just saved me a hunk of trouble — she's harder to find than you might think. So I figure the least I can do is to pay you out of what she woulda paid you. Then we call it quits. That way I walk, you get to live, and everybody's happy, like little clams." He took out a packet of C-notes. "This cover it?"

I stared at the body. I shook my head.

"No?" His eyebrow — the skeptical one — registered mild surprise. "So what do I owe you."

I shook it again, from the pit of misery.

"Nothing. You don't owe us nothing. We was workin' for free."

~ *The End* ~

MURPHY GETS LAID

So I'm looking down sort of speculatively, and she's kind of lying back and relaxing things, in a way that seems to say: Help yourself!

It didn't taste as great as you might think — not much flavor to these things, really, when you get right down to it (when you go right down on it) — sort of like fresh mozzarella that way, everybody likes it well enough but you can't really compare it to, say, like, lasagna, except maybe in ways that wouldn't bear comparison. But anyhow, the gesture was appreciated on both sides. And now that we had the preliminaries out of the way, and everybody was by now quite obviously ready for the main course, we moved on to more of what the Lord had in mind when he made me *this* way and her *that* way.

Course, He also had in mind that we'd be married. Oh well. Chalk up another for the confessional. Really, I ought to keep a notebook.

META-MURPHY MATERIALS

Following are stories and a poem which explore
alternative facets of the world of the Murphy brothers.

LOST AND FOUND

"This Jack, joke, poor potsherd, patch, matchwood,
immortal diamond
       Is immortal diamond."
— Hopkins, Heraclitean Fire

To an objective observer, which Murphy was not, the girl would have to have been described as tall, even angular. The color of her eyes, to the extent that this detail can be reconstructed, was green. Murphy himself could not have stated this with certainty, for all his training in the arts of observation. Neither later, as the events would be recalled through a veil of tears, nor even at the time. He'd had, in fact, a hard time focusing on her; her image wavered, like a flame.

She had come to his office, a second-floor walkup, in the usual fashion, unannounced and off the street. Her coming had been unheralded by any major earthquakes or strange signs in the sky. But still, as she stood before him now in a simple skirt and ... some kind of top ... and probably shoes, as she stood there a long or a short while not speaking, Murphy was not sure.

"You're ... a private investigator," she asked or stated at last, in any case simply verifying the information on the faded sign below, out front, which indicated that Murphy, together with his brother, was indeed of that profession.

He waved her to a chair, not answering, turning aside as though preoccupied. He wasn't sure, but there was something about her. He examined his fingernails, which for a time seemed the best bet to concentrate on without let-up till the danger passed, but after a time his mind bled back to the matter at hand. He wasn't sure it was resistible. She sat down.

He glanced at her, wincing, or barely refraining from wincing, and looked away, and his hand was going across his (to the touch) ill-shaven upper lip, wiping a new dew of moisture away. "I *was*," he said. "I'm, hmm, thinking of getting out of it. Actually I'm thinking of taking up tax-return preparation, run a little service; and here it is only June. So you probably don't …"

"So *you* probably don't have a lot of business yet, right?" she said with a smile. "No look, it's okay. But if you don't feel you've gotten rusty yet, there's a little detecting you could do for me. If you want to."

Murphy nodded; Murphy looked down. Focused briefly with complete clarity on a random spot on the floor, inventorying its contents of (1) Camel butt and (2) sundry dust particles, snowflake-like in their infinite variety; then faded out and forgot about it and looked up a little and said, or found himself saying, "I actually do want to."

And then from out of nowhere she smiled at him: not a smile of gratitude, or not, who knows what, just one of those not even thinking about it just like a breeze blowing freely blowing openings in the clouds — and Murphy fell into it, moaning, it crashed around his ears loud-soundlessly like a huge wave. He felt a sickness, a very old one. Had it ever been this piercing, and this, Jesus, this *fast*? Over like, nothing? A what, a look? Murphy get a grip on yourself.

He managed to say, although hoarse, forming his words very carefully: "What/ - would/ - be/ - the/ - nature/ - of/ - this/ - case."

Possibly (within her) the faintest of taken-abackness at the hint of strain and something held back, the tone not of question but resignation. But going forward without a hitch. She: "Some time ago I suffered a burglary. I lost a diamond ring, by far the most precious thing I had, and irreplaceable. I wonder if you could see if you could find it for me."

This he had not expected. He felt dismay, several levels of dismay. "Lady, lady, a thing like that, that's hard to get back."

A nod, a little-girl bravery and grown-up frown. "I know. But I have to try. To keep trying."

Nodding, pacing, yes, yes, he understood *that* well enough. But he also knew that, in all decency and all honesty, he should not take the case.

He lifted his eyes like barbells and looked up at her and kept his eyes on her, front and center, though they faded to mist. "I'll do it. Terms, say five hundred if I find it, nothing otherwise."

Little pursed lips for an instant. "You'll want expenses, though. A retainer. It will involve some travel. I lived back over across the river at the time it happened. Can you handle that?"

He almost laughed. He wanted to say: Lady, I would go to the ends of the earth for you, through the briars of the forest, through the fire of flame, to the black brick cliff at the edge of the world, and if need be fall off. What he said was: "That won't be a problem."

She opened her pocketbook. He averted his gaze. "So what are your — usual rates?"

He actually did laugh a little, silently. His *usual, rates*! He had no idea, not the faintest idea in hell.

She left a twenty on the table and he nodded and she described (in general terms) the missing item and he nodded and she left.

Time passed, though nothing happened, and after a while Joey came in, back from the bars and the barnyards, back from the wide outside.

"Heyya Murphy good brother, what's 'at twenty I see? 'Old Hickory' Andrew Jackson, a welcome face. We got a customer?"

"Hm? Oh, no." Joey waited. "Or I mean, yeah. Just a little — nothing big."

Joey shifted his weight around and cracked his knuckles and went and got a beer from the fridge. "No missing person this time, hah?" He sucked the foam and considered. "That'll be a change."

"No well, not exactly. Actually just some stolen property — "

Joey shot a look at him of surprise and no pleasure. "No, but hey, Murphy, a mug's game. Nobody hardly gets stolen property back in this town. Whaddaya ..."

"No well, yeah, right, but she got like serial numbers and stuff, plus some payment upfront with no contingency ..."

"Serial numbers, what like, a car, or what?"

"Yeh, something like that. Anyhow maybe I'll find some of it, won't spend too much time on it, and like there's nothing else on our plate right now."

Joey sipped and, harboring his mouthful, considered his head from side to side. "Yeh well, maybe. You want I track half the items, you take half?"

"No no no! I mean there's not much. No, shit, forget it, I'll take care of it. You just — whyncha see you can drum up some business down around the station house."

"Yeahhh, well ... See if I can drum up some business down at Mama Rosa's. See ya in a while." Joey, losing interest, ambled out.

Murphy began the quest that night, not waiting for a sign or for the dawn. He moved in whispers through the sides of the streets, motioning to figures, stuffing bills into sagging jacket pockets, questioning, seeking hints from blank faces, seeking leads from dead ends. Finally, penniless, he just walked and wondered, until the sun struggled up from behind the tenements and garbage cans.

Murphy came back to the apartment and threw his clothes to the side and took a blindingly hot shower for a long, long time.

The next day, things went a little better. Perhaps just from exhaustion, Murphy had calmed down.

He made a list of all the pawn shops in the city and surrounding areas, and stores selling used jewelry. The rest was just shoe leather. With the stub of a pencil he checked off each address after he had examined their holdings. One by one, he drew a blank.

Back at the office, he asked Joey had anyone called.

"Yeh Sam called, and that Resnick guy, plus someone who says we owe him money, and ..."

He rattled off a few more names but Murphy didn't hear them. "What I mean is, did anyone *special* call?"

"Anyone ... special."

"Yeh. Anyone. *Extra* special."

Joey shook his head dubiously. "No, Murphy, no one like that."

Murphy, magical Murphy, magical Murphy in Murphyland. He glides, he slides, he discovers things. Secrets are not safe from him. They recline sighing, widening their thighs.

Murphy was wise to the ways of the street. He knew the smell of it. And now he almost imagined he could detect that diamond by some inner sense; though even more than money, a diamond has no odor. Perhaps he was detecting some pocket of vacuum in the general riot of all-pervading smells.

Suddenly his body tensed as he spotted a man in a dark suit and a homburg walk quickly out of a jewelry store and turn smartly down Forty-Seventh Street, walking away from him. Murphy eased out of the doorway where he'd been stationed and began to follow the man at a natural pace. The man's step seemed to quicken and Murphy lengthened his stride but did not quicken his pace. Soon they were moving at a pretty good clip, weaving among the mostly oncoming pedestrian traffic and just making the lights — the homburg getting the tail end of the green, Murphy the tail end of the yellow. The man turned down a side street and suddenly looked back; Murphy fortunately had not yet turned and simply continued across the street, then doubled back, now with his own hat discarded and his collar turned up. The man was still in sight, about half-way down the block.

Murphy was about thirty feet away when the man stopped and started to turn. Murphy just had time to step back into an areaway, where he could observe from the shadows. The man was rapping lightly at a door or perhaps ringing a buzzer. Time passed. The door opened and, apparently without a word being exchanged, a small package was passed out. The man nodded, rather curtly, and began quickly to retrace his steps, coming now towards the place where Murphy lay in wait.

He stepped out in front of him like a hammer coming down, grabbed both lapels and stood him up so straight against the brownstone wall that the man, a couple of inches Murphy's junior in height, was now exactly as tall as Murphy. They locked eyes. Neither spoke. Slowly Murphy's grip relaxed, and gradually his shoulders sagged.

"It isn't you," he acknowledged, hanging his head.

"No," said the man, "it isn't me."

And yet, thought Murphy, turning the incident over in his mind at the lunch counter an hour later, and yet there is something that is not right. Someone was playing him for a fool.

He slowly spun around on his stool and looked out through the dirt-streaked window with its backwards letters and saw the people passing by, to the left, to the right, to the left, to the right. All coming from somewhere and going somewhere else. One of them knowing what Murphy needed to know.

He slid off the stool, left some bills that would cover the tab and the tip, and headed out into the slicing sunlight. He squinted, looking up street and down. Which way had he gone? He stood some time in indecision, fitfully considering his options. And then again his instincts snapped awake, as a runt of a man, a sharp dresser, passed rapidly before him, hand in his right jacket pocket. Murphy smelled a rat.

He moved after him, not even trying to disguise the pursuit. The runt broke into a run. Murphy followed suit but the runt was fast on his feet and Murphy soon was breathing hard, a bear pursuing a rabbit.

A squad car passed along a side street just as the runt was about to cross, and ingrained habit caused him to instantly slow his pace and casually turn his back and sort of amble in some other direction and that was enough for Murphy to catch up. He wasted no time on formalities.

"Plainclothes!" he barked, flashing his P.I. badge too quickly to be distinguished from anything else, and pushed the man backwards into an alley lit by a single slant of sunlight. The runt offered no resistance. Murphy began systematically to toss him, setting out the contents of innumerable pockets onto the lids of the trash cans beside them. All the detritus of an untidy life: most of it legal, whether or not it was legally come by, and none of it what Murphy was after.

"All right, beat it," he said, and his victim made no argument.

Back on the street, Murphy bit the back of his hand in puzzlement, squinting at the sun.

Time passed. Murphy passed with it. Increasingly baffled and intense.

Surely she must be wondering what the progress was by now. He checked the answering machine, he checked the mail. And then, she appeared, as in a vision.

Murphy stammered. "You never even told me your name."

Silence.

"Well — How can I know you?"

"Sola Gratia."

"Oh! Well okay then, Miss, uh, Miss Gratia. I'm, well, I'm like, working on it. Got some hunches, got a few leads." He waited for her response to his clumsy lies.

She was gone.

All right, okay, time to call in a few chits. Maybe even to go into deficit.

Murphy knew a certain fence, who had once given him information in the past, though not on any of the fence's clients. It was a long shot, and a hard sell, but Murphy was running out of options.

They met at some distance from the fence's usual place of business, and Murphy got right to the point. Laid out the case, described the goods, stated what he was offering in the case of compliance and hinting what he was threatening in the opposite case.

"What, you crazy?" said the fence, not impressed. "A loose stone? They're not going to keep it in the ring, that'll be melted. You can't trace a thing like that."

"But you might know, you must know, tell me anyone who has taken diamonds."

"You're crazy, Murphy."

Murphy bared his teeth, and unleashed an attack that afterwards left him dizzy and frightened. Really he seemed to be losing it. And yet, the guy was holding out on him! Murphy left, shivering and sick.

He lay on his back on an unmade bed, staring sightlessly up at the ceiling very far away, turning things over and over in his mind.

The phone rang. He shrank back, fearing it might be her.

Several times it rang during the day. He stayed in a corner of the room.

And then at some time in the time of the night, he found himself with the phone in his hand. It was her.

"Mr. Murphy?"

He nodded.

"Hope it isn't too late. I tried calling earlier."

He nodded again.

"Any luck so far?"

He whispered an answer, laid the handset in the cradle like a leaf on a bank of snow.

Murphy made it through the days, unshorn, unshaven, scanning the personals, taking notes, making phone calls, trying to piece it all together.

Joey idled by.

"Slice?"

"Uh — no thanks, Joey."

Joey shrugged and was gone.

It was time for drastic action. He would get it for her, whatever it took.

He paced all afternoon across the street from one of the better jewelry stores. Dusk fell gently. At closing time the clerk stepped forward and reversed the OPEN sign, but Murphy already had his foot in the door.

He showed the clerk his gun, just briefly, not threatening, simply establishing a fact.

"Gimme your best diamond."

The clerk was slender, immaculately tailored and coiffed, but now he was sweating around the eyes, sweating on his lip, sweating in his silk drawers. He handed Murphy a large trayful. "Here, take them. Just remain calm."

Murphy looked at the trayful in confusion and dismay. "Whadaya, whadoo I want widdiss, ya tryina — which is the best?"

The clerk is baffled, fades out, then slowly fades in again. "You don't ... you don't want them all?"

"Whaddoo ... I ... whadaya! Just, which is the *best*!"

A sort of improvised comprehension and veiled slyness enter the salesman's face. The sweat begins to dry.

"Just as you say, sir. Would this be for an engagement or for society wear? Quite the most fashionable cut at public functions this season is this one here, an elegant yet individual conception of — "

"Stow it, I want the *best*, just the *best*!"

Suddenly emotionless. "That would be this one, right here."

Murphy dumps what money he has, not much, takes the stone and splits.

Murphy went down to the docks and paced, rolling the gem around in his hand.

What a fraud. She would see right through it. Furious with himself, he hurled the stone as far as he could, into the black waters of the bay.

In his mind he moved towards her suddenly, immobile, like the speed of light in a vacuum, when it doesn't know which way to go.

Finally Joey confronted him, darkly furious. "Murphy, you been cheatin' on me. You been steppin' out. Outside a the line."

Normally a hard word from his brother would cut him to the quick. And even now, Murphy felt bad about it, but he is unable to feel about it the way he would feel, were his heart at his own disposal.

More time, more time. If only he had *more time*.

He had all the time in the world. Time to burn, time in spades. And it wasn't enough.

She called, or he called her. It was the final call.

He confessed his failure. She seemed not to take it hard. She began to take her leave but suddenly he interrupted her, his voice taking on an unbearable urgency.

"Lady lady, I'm not just a P.I., you know. Not at all. I can *serve*. No no, please listen. I can do other things for you. Everything, anything. Fix your car, do your taxes. Grow your garden, wash your windows. Carry your bags, protect you from the sun, shield you from shadows. Please, anything. I can go on trips, run errands for you. *Please*. I can go to the market: for eggs. I can go to the store: for milk."

He listened in silence, to the silence, crackling immensely across acres of empty space. And then he heard the click as she hung up forever, and vanished vastly and forever from his unimagined life.

Silence. The roaring, deafening silence of the dial tone.

He closed his eyes down hard on the heat, and his teeth sank deep, into his fist, sweet, deep, as sweet and deep as ice-cream. And then subsided. For in the layers upon layers of the darkness, with a clarity that was like forgiveness, he could see the diamond, where it lay, restored to her keeping, as bright as day.

~ The End ~

The Temptation of Murphy, or: Dead Men Don't Talk Back

Maybe you folks got it all wrong. You see, usually, I'm writing up my case-files, we start out from hunger, and then comes a knock. You only been with us about ten minutes when, Wham, we got ourselves a case. So you might get the impression that things are always hopping down at Murphy's, like the White Castle at Grand Central.

Well, *duh. Course* I start when the good stuff starts, the parts with guns and dames, and those close calls and narrow escapes, that has made the name of Murphy a byword in bars all over town. And *natch* I don't linger over the days when nothing much happened, just drinking, re-reading the funny-papers, tossing out unpaid bills. Fact a the matter: Whole weeks can go by without a nibble. Whole months can go by without a bite.

Like right now, things are getting a bit low in the larder; so I summon my trusty assistant.

"Require an update on our holdings in the three basic food-groups: Pop-tarts, and Camels, and Mickey's Big Mouth. Corporal Joey, in your capacity as quartermaster, present your report."

"Well we're fixed fine for Mickeys, just got in a new shipment, fell off a truck. Pop-tarts holding steady at next to nothing. And Camels ... " Words fail him, and he holds forth something crumpled and sad.

I peer down into it, like peering down a wishing-well, that never grants wishes.

We're down to our last Camel – not counting the loose tobacco at the bottom of the pack (a blend of the finest Domestic and Turkish varieties, now blended more intimately than usual), that falls out the ends of the no-filters, that you might in principle scrape together and either chew or snort. We'd have to break this one in half, each of us just smoke it down and savor it, right down to the singed fingers and scorched lips.

So it's a cinch I gotta scare up some scratch, some how, some way. So I head down to Sam the Pawnie's; he already got our toaster – been back and forth so often, he wound up naming it, like a pet — but something will come to me. Heck, I reflect – it's a sunny day, not too much breeze ... What do I need this shirt for?

So I walk in whistling, with my bright idea.

"Pawn a shirt, Sammy." Whistling, rocking back and forth on my shoes (they're next), feeling pretty good, considering.

Sammy's been in this business for forty years. Seen 'em come and seen 'em go – go, mostly. Knows it all like the back of his hairy big hand, quote you prices right out of memory, really knows the ropes.

But this time, he shakes his head. "People don't really ... *pawn — shirts*, Murphy."

"Whaddaya whaddaya. Great shirt. Been good to me these past ten years."

"Yeh, looks it. But what do I do, you don't pay back the loan, I gotta sell it? Who's gonna buy it?"

"A wino might."

"And pay with what?"

"With – with empties."

"*Mur*-phy-y-y ... I already got an overflow of empties, what you pawned. Be reasonable, Murphy. Here, look, I'll lend you a fiver, just as a friend. But keep your shirt on."

So I go home feeling pretty good again. The fiver turns into a couple of slices, one for me one for Joey, and they taste real good until they're gone.

Then I get to thinking: Maybe we're going about this whole thing all wrong. Stead of turning stuff down, maybe we oughta *specialize* in divorce cases — drum up some business with billboards, big letters: "YOUR SPOUSE SUX" and "LOSE THAT LOSER" and "DITCH THAT BITCH." Soon, we would be rich beyond the dreams of Avarice. And of Gluttony, and of Envy, and of Sloth ...

So I'm working out the angles, thinking all the custom you might get with just a few anonymous letters, some stolen panties ... the imagination reels.

And then I draw up short and think, Who ordered *that*? Sometimes you wonder what bus such thoughts rode in on, when you're dreaming about what-all you'd like to do with some broad that you fancy, or what you'd like to do *to* some bloke that you don't. I figured I'd better go wash out my grey cells with soap.

Days pass. Supplies are running out. Even the Mickey's has dwindled faster than we had ever thought possible. And finally, we're down to just one last Pop-tart. Toaster long pawned, what to do? Plus now we're up against a case of Lifeboat Ethics: do we smoke our last cigarette, or use it to heat up the pop-tart? Case is moot, though, we're out of matches. Used to be, you'd get 'em free, but now they're hard to find, or they charge for 'em, since most of the Quality got lighters.

"What say we just stick it out in the sun for a while?"

So we set it on the ledge for a spell, and go work the crossword puzzle; but then a stray dog comes along and wolfs it down.

I looked sadly at the spot where the pop-tart used to be: the Pop-Tart that Might Have Been.

"This might be the bottom, Joey."

"No, a guy might go lower. We might of been lawyers."

Well, heck. "Doesn't matter. Wasn't hungry anyway."

"Me neither. What's hunger?"

"Forget what it even feels like, done plain forgot the meaning of the word. ... Some times get kinda ... *thirsty*, though ... "

And then, just then – we don't hear a knock, we don't hear nothing. But we notice now a figure standing over us, maybe been standing that way for some time.

"You Murphy?"

"Me and Joey."

"And do you take just any assignment that comes along?"

"Sure we do. Minus certain exceptions. You want me to repo a ring from the wife what you dumped, then bump her off, it's no go."

"Naw ... heck ... She can keep the ring ... — Just kidding." Then he got serious again. "I notice you cleared your calendar in advance of my coming. That's a good sign."

"Yeh, we're free as a couple of jailbirds, saying goes."

"Good, fine." He stretches, and starts to pace. "I've got a little job for you boys," he says, walking up and down, going to and fro in the earth. "One that's—"

"—strickly –"

"—strictly on the up-'n- up."

"Just like I like 'em," I mutter.

"And I'll pay you both – well, I might pay you and I might not: you know how these things go."

"That we do, oh, that we do."

"It involves a jane."

"It usually do."

"And a man with a past."

I'm listening; go on.

"And a man with no future – no future at all."

I stiffen. "No reference to current company, I trust."

"None."

I nod him go on.

"And it ties in with ... with a man with no name."

I nod bitterly. Just my luck.

"The jane disappeared some time ago, without a trace. We reckon she linked up with the Man with a Past. But now the Man with No Future is gunning for them: and if you two don't get there ahead of him, it's a cinch that both wind up dead."

I didn't like the odds. "And the Man with No Name?"

The stranger just gave a tight smile, and shook his head.

He went on to give the particulars of the case: Who did what to whom when, back in Shanghai; who was tied in with whomever, though nothing could be proved; and which parties stood most to gain in the aftermath of the Brandywire Affair. I won't bore you with the details – I wrote it all down.

After he's gone, Joey stares at me, something's occurred to him. "Hey Murphy – we never even asked the name of our client?"

Bitterly: "Whaddaya wanna know 'is *name* for, Joey? *You* know who he is."

—

[Middle section goes here. Stuff happens, etc.]

—

Eyes narrowed, the cigarette gently trembling, slowly, slowly sucking in smoke.

"So, how you figure *that* angle, huh?"

—

[… more stuff …]

—

"Way I figure, guy's got about six chances in this life. You blow five of them – just one left."

—

"Not sure this case is been worth it, y'know? Six dead so far … "

"Ya gotta play the cards you got dealt."

—

"Hey, Blackie — lookin' back on it – ya woulda killed him the same way, *that* way, or some *other* way?"

Eyes glowing. "Oh ... if only I had it to do over again... "

—

[Other stuff; and then the climax:]

—

... The spent cigarette jogged little bits up and down, while he spoke from the side of his mouth.

"So you thought you were smart, walking out on us like that."

I shifted my gun to the other hand.

He reached for his own; but I was too quick:

I blasted the Man with a Past.

[...]

So when the case was all over, me and Joey kicked back, lazing around in a couple of lawn chairs, out on the sidewalk, in front of the dump. Didn't make a dime, but, boy-y, did we have fun. More fun nor a barrel of ...

"Monkeys," said Joey.

"*Baby* monkeys," I said.

"Piglets."

"Aardvarks."

" ... Hamsters!"

" ... *Baby* hamsters!"

He sighed, and conceded the contest. "Aw, Murphy: You know I can't top that."

MURPHY OUTLINES HIS THEORY OF THE CLASS DAME

"Nice tits: that's class.

Tight ass: that's class too.

Clothes — Yeh, sure, clothes. Whatever.

Personality? Yeh, she can have some of that. Just not too much of it. I mean, enough's enough."

MURPHY: AN INTRODUCTION

The Boss takes the cigar out of his face and leans forward, genuinely incredulous.

"No wait — no wait. Help me t'understand, here. I come to you, in all sincerity, and I offer you my business. Me! *My* business. Now it pays well, very well — just the budget for these cigars, for a week, could buy up this whole freakin' rat-hole you live in, what you call your ... 'office'. But that's not the point. Not the point at all."

Murphy shook his head, but in agreement: Not the point at all.

"Point is: I offer you — *I, me*, offer you, *you* ..." (a withering look here) "**my-y** business! I mean, me, I got my honor here."

Murphy thinks: That what you call it?

"An' it's like: *if* — and this would never happen, I'm a generous guy, just part of my nature, can't help it, a generous guy — but all I'm sayin' is: *if*, I was to come to you, and say: You. Do this: for me. As a personal favor. Y'know? Nine guys outa ten — wait, ninety-nine guys out of a hundred — crap. Solly; Solly, you're the math guy, gimme some figures here."

Toneless, obliging: "Nine hundred and ninety-nine thousand, nine hundred and ninety-nine, ... out of an even million."

"Yeh — that! What he said! Nine ... *you* heard it, ninededy ninededy fuckyourmother *whatever*, these guys say: Yes, sir. Thank you, sir. It would be a pleasure, sir. It would be an — *honor*, sir. Thank you, thank you, thank you sir, it shall be done; and if it is, sir, not too presumptuous, sir, sir — would you permit us to maybe, suck your ... O we know we are not worthy of any actual *body* part, sir; but might we be permitted to suck your shoe? Or maybe just your footprint, or the butt that your shoe just crushed?"

Murphy shrugged. "No argument from me on that."

A snort. "Good! Good. You're learning."

(Murphy: No I'm not.)

"Yet but: *you*! You think you're too good for my business — Are you too good for my business?"

"Nope. Not one bit. Hard to find something I'm too good for."

"Okay good! All right we're getting somewhere! So then: Why: Won't: You: Take my *business*???!!!"

Again the shrug — what other gesture fits? "Nothin' personal, it's just: I don't do divorce cases."

Measured tones: "You don't do divorce cases."

"Right. That. What you said."

Amazement. Looking right and left to his henchmen, but they can't figure it either.

"You don't do — Listen, my friend. You do this case, that's the last case you ever have to *do*. Capisc'? You retire on your earnings, retire on your winnings, never have to do a case again — No more divorce! No more ...

Anything else the little princess would rather not touch?"

Murphy mumbled: "Repo. Don't do repo, either."

"Ahh ... repo, no repo. — All right my little Lemon Flower ... So why you don't take my nice divorce case, and then retire for life. What are you ... maybe ... retarded?"

"No, not really. No Einstein, but not retarded."

"Okay, now we gettin' somewheres. Rule out: Retarded. Guy's not retarded. So what, you like ... swore some holy *vow-w*, somewhere, you don't do divorce cases?"

"Nope. No vow."

"So ... be a sport, here; help me understand here: *Why* ... do you not ... '*do*' ... divorce cases?"

And here, Mr. Murphy stood once again on solid ground. "No reason I could put into words. I just *don't*."

Bafflement, silence. Open palms tossed wide to the sides in the old "Don't ask *me*" gesture; exchanged glances; perhaps an index-finger twirled little spirals beside a temple, on the part of one of the lower-downs.

Suddenly an idea occurs to The Boss. Insight spreads over his face like a fart being slowly released from a sphincter. "O-oh ... waitaminit ... You don't — don't tell me ... You don't ..." (he stifles a snicker) "you don't like, believe in like ..." (complicitous glances tossed back and forth among the henchmen, laughter stifled like a fart restrained) "believe in like ..." (the

215

mirth is almost too much; tears streaming from the sides of eyes) " … in like … *GOD*, do you???!!!"

And Murphy does not right away answer. He frowns and thinks. Finally he says, simply: "That's a big question, and I'm a small man. Hafta take a rain check on that one." Observing the astonished silence of everyone else in the room, Murphy goes on. "But what I do believe in — I mean, seeing as how you ask — believe in, even more than seeing this beer bottle here," he says, casually picking one up, "is … short words, big idea: Free Will. And like even those, whatever you call 'em, those ninety-nine guys: they were maybe scared spitless, what you'd do to them, they didn't do what you said; but even so, they did have that one thing that you can't take away, even if they're in chains."

The face of the Boss registered a look of genuine alarm. He began to try a new tack, a new tone. "An amusing argument. If you choose to believe in that childish fiction, that's no concern of mine. But to demonstrate the sincerity of my offer, I shall make a notable exception in your case: Should you unwisely decline my offer, I'll … do nothing to you. You can walk away. Instead, I am asking you to accept it out of your — as you so quaintly put it — your own 'free will': as a friend."

Murphy, lost in thought, tapped his palm absent-mindedly with the bottle. He labored to make his meaning plain — plain mainly to himself, for he was only just now getting clear on this.

"Yeh, it's absurd all right — no argument there. But it's real — like this." Again he brandished the bottle, which had come to play, in this interview, the role traditionally assigned to the proverbial coffee cup in more philosophical discourse. "Lemme give y'an example. Mostly, we do what we like to do, or something that, even if we don't like it at the time, gonna bring us something we do like, later on (just not too long later on). But, *sometimes*, we do something that's no fun, and that is only gonna cause us a world of pain, but it's the right thing to do, and we do it — and not on impulse, either. We think about it, think about it, think some more, and then we ... *Do* it," said Murphy, bringing the beer bottle crashing down on the forehead of The Boss, the henchman too astonished — too out of their element, really — to react at first. Then they sprang, and pinned his arms, and looked wildly to their employer for guidance; yet no guidance came, from within the whirlwind of roars, which seemed to stem, beyond any superficial skin-injuries, from echoing depths below.

"And I guess now," said Murphy, on the same tone as before, "I guess now you're probably really mad at me."

~ *The End* ~

MURPHY MEETS THE MAGISTERIUM

Benedicta tu in mulieribus
— old folksong

It was around the time of the Huntfire Case, that Murphy became, albeit briefly, a Buddhist.

The circumstances were these. Material conditions had been unusually pinched, and the Murphy Brothers were even more than usually limited in their choice of cuisine: in particular, they were unable to afford hamburgers. So Murphy figured, long's he was missing out on meat, he might as well get credit for it: and he'd heard tell as how those Buddhist folks were vegetarians by trade. So he became a Buddhist.

The idea had been suggested to him fortuitously, when, munching his morning crispies (now alas with water rather than milk), he spotted a blurb on the box, peddling a new religion. Actually several different ones, you could take your pick; it was like a salad bar, with cuisine from Southern California, Northern Tibet, even this novelty-religion being pushed by a pudgy little two-foot-tall dog. But the one that caught his eye was: *Buddhist*. Partly because he had indeed heard the word before, so that it was to that extent comfortingly familiar; partly because it was so exotically impossible to spell, even though it's not at all difficult to pronounce — I mean, it rhymes with "nudist." (And, he thought, reflectively munching his soggy mush, with not much else; which must make it difficult for Buddhist poets to come up with jingles celebrating their faith.)

Now, a conversion is not a thing to be undertaken lightly. The box did not promise that you could become a Buddhist simply by wishing it were so. Instead, you had to scissors out the appropriate rectangle, sign your name solemnly promising etc etc, and mail it in along with five dollars in American pennies to an address in the Cayman Islands. Which Murphy did.

By return mail came an official certificate, in an ornate font and ornate language that by themselves were worth the price of admission, testifying that Michael Xavier Murphy, being of sound mind or at least anyhow of sound body, is hereby and by these presents officially and as a matter of both theology and law, now fully and finally a Buddhist.

Murphy read this with satisfaction and carefully folded the document and placed it in his right rear trousers pocket, to be available for authentication should anyone at any time have the brass balls to doubt his Buddhist bona fides.

The first test came early. Round about getting on lunchtime, Murphy and Joey sauntered out into the gladsome air of a spring morn. Sunlight glittered upon the fire hydrants, and twinkled amid the jets of water which, in this neighborhood, normally issue playfully from the vents. Pairs of shoes, joined by laces as though in matrimony, hung from the phone wires where otherwise birds might perch.

"Man!" said Murphy, overcome with joie de vivre. "What a nice day — I mean, from a Buddhist perspective."

They soon were passing the familiar establishment of Happy's Hamburgers, the scene of many memories. Already the alluring aroma of diced onions goldening on a griddle, being groomed to adorn their beefburger bride, herself being prepared to perfection and placed softly upon a toasted bun, beguiled their nostrils with come-hither fingers of fragrance. But this time, instead of standing, nose pressed to the glass, Murphy waved an airy paw, didn't pause in his stride, and snorted, "Cheece! How can people eat such treyf?"

Being short of the price of a slice, they figured they'd drop by Eddie's, he should be up by now. Nice guy, generous guy, had a wet-bar right in his basement, a basement that doubled as his ground floor and penthouse; and often there would still be a few pretzels left over from the previous night's revelries, enough to provide a spartan but satisfying meal.

Eddie greeted them warmly, tugging on his T-shirt, and reaching for his first cigarette of the day. But, ever the perfect host, he offered the pack to Murphy first.

Murphy had had nothing to eat or drink that day, so he wasn't really up for a smoke. Plus the pack Eddie was extending, was not his brand. I mean they were o-

kay, they didn't have any fancy-ass filters on 'em or any freaking menthol in 'em; but they weren't his brand. Which he was anyhow out of; but still. What say let's turn this lemon into lemonade.

He considered hard; then said:

"Buddhists don't smoke."

Eddie threw his head back and laughed. "Oh they *don't*, don't they? Well I'll be damned!"

Murphy glowered. "You just might be. — Buddhists don't cuss."

Eddie still half laughing, turned aside and went over to his basement wet-bar. "Oh, Murphy, you're one too many for me. Suit yourself. — Say, look, it's almost noon. Join me in a brew?"

Eddie pulled the tab on the tap of a keg standing tall and bulgy on top of his bar. From this there issued a stream of foam, soon going golden. The glistening liquid slowly mounted the sides of the thick pint glass, rising ever higher until it finally breached the brim.

Eddie held out the offering invitingly. "Only … I guess you Buddhist guys don't drink either, huh."

Murphy considered. Already dew was pearling upon the cool sides of the mug. His stomach grumbled consent. But Murphy, the stern theologian, did not give up so easily as that. He considered some more, in a brown study; but at length, his features relaxed.

"Well see now, there's a coupla different types of us Buddhists. There's the old hardcore-hardshell-hardline kind, that's the kind you probably heard about, they're the old *Two-Seed-in-the-Spirit* Buddhists, *they* don't touch a drop. But then you got your other kind, and that's *my* kind, see? And *they* got a different philosophy altogether, comes straight from Outer India; and *they* say, 'tain't but the *one* seed there in the spirit, and not *two*. And *they* drink whatever they like, *whenever* they like, and as much as it darn well suits them."

He grabbed the tankard with his fat right hand, and took a long tug, from its head of foam like a froth of philosophy.

Their thirst slaked, and a good time having been had by all, the Murphys returned to their operational headquarters, with *one* of their appetites satisfied at least. They paused a moment to admire the sign out front:

MURPHY BROS. — PRIVATE INVESTIGATORS — DISCRETION ASSURED.

Beneath which Murphy had carefully inked: "BUDDHIST STUFF A SPECIALTY." Then they went upstairs to await their first client of the day.

Which in this case would equally be their first client of the month. And the month itself had not much oomph left in it — just one more ragged rectangle to tear off the day-page blotter, O come, O do come, don't leave us to languish, all alone in the lurch; another shut-out month like the last one, we may have to shut up shop.

And then it came — that click-click-click of the high heels of destiny coming down the sidewalk. The click-click comes quickly, slowing as the feet must negotiate some obstacle on the path, then resuming their pace. The pace of fate.

Silently, accepting what must happen, the Murphy brothers wait, head bowed. A trip-trip-trip on the bare wooden stairs, and then a knock: a soft, tentative knock.

As usual, Joey opens the door and shows the prospective client in, waving her to a chair. But as unusual, Joey does not immediately turn the case over to Murphy, who, to Joey's surprise, is now sitting over in the corner, more or less in lotus position (nearabouts as makes no difference), eyes closed or almost so, making little circles with his thumb and finger, like they're these little radio antennas and he's going to pick up some sort of wisdom broadcasts from Tibet. The dame — a dame indeed it is — shoots Joey a questioning look, but he just shrugs. Nothing for it, she launches into it.

"I have come to see you about a — a missing — " her throat catches.

"About a man," says Joey kindly. "A man who's missing from your life."

"That's right!" she exclaims, too suddenly re-enthused to dwell at all at what might have been surprise. "He walked out — He disappeared. Just like that! He disappeared."

"Without a trace," said Joey, nodding. "Yes, we've seen that kind of thing before."

"Is it ... the kind of thing you guys can handle?"

Joey spreads his hands. "Mostly, the only kind of case we ever get."

"And, if I might inquire ... I'm not very well-off, but ... What are your rates?"

Joey shook his head with a sigh, feeling all the weariness of the world. "Rates, rates ... we'll maybe talk about that later. When the time is right. Don't worry — you can afford it." He didn't add: It's academic anyway. We almost never actually get paid.

He went over to the sink, found a reasonably clean jelly-jar, and brought her some cold water from the tap.

"Here you go; do you good. Whyncha just begin at the beginning."

She took a sip and composed herself, wriggled just a little to settle herself in the chair; and then began, in a small, clear voice.

"My husband and I had been happy for some time. We were ... reasonably prosperous. I mean, nothing fancy, but nothing that should have driven him to seek another ... a second source of income. He had a steady job, um, somewhere in the city. But with time, he began spending more time at work.

"I asked him about it one evening and he just grunted and shrugged it off. Said some stuff sometimes kept him late. So I let it rest; but when next week he didn't come home for dinner, three times in a row, I called his office: and he wasn't there.

"I confronted him, he was gruff and evasive. And then the possibility began to dawn on me: He had a second job. Something he couldn't tell me about. Something secret. Something for the government, or — ? I hoped to heaven it wasn't anything worse than that.

"My fears were soon confirmed. He began to stay away for whole weeks at a time. 'Business trips', he said, but he returned distracted and very tired, as though he had been in some danger. A woman just knows this, when she loves a man: I could tell that something was weighing on his mind. Something deep, something secret. I began to fear he was being sent on missions that might end badly for us both."

This was starting to get complicated. Joey looked around for a notepad, take some of this stuff down; but, seeing none, and not wishing to miss a word of the narrative, which was beginning to take on a strange lilt of its own, he returned to giving her his full attention.

"Evidence continued to pile up — it all fit. He began to receive letters in an unfamiliar hand. The phone would ring, twice; then nothing. Obviously some sort of code.

"The climax came one Tuesday night. Roger had not come home. The phone rang and this time I grabbed it before it could ring again. A woman's voice said, 'Roger?' I said, biting off my words: Here's not here; and just who are you. After a pause, the woman replied calmly, with a professional air: 'Tell him East Berlin, Alexanderplatz, three a.m. Come alone. You will receive instructions.' Then she hung up.

"For a moment I was stunned; then I realized what must have happened. She had somehow got her wires crossed, and had mistaken me for one of his agents — or maybe his Control!"

She spoke more hurried now, an unclarity coming into her voice.

"I was desperate to make contact with him. I knew that his life was in danger — and with his life, my happiness for all time! I didn't care what extra money he might be bringing in, I didn't care — Nothing could ever replace him for me!"

She halted, repressed a sob. Then spoke up again, bravely.

"I never saw him again. No letter, no phone call, not even a ransom note. And from that day ...

And then they noticed that Murphy, still motionless, was murmuring, softly, to himself. "Lady, lady, lady, lady, ..." They exchanged glances, but did not interrupt.

"Lady, O Lady," he said, a little louder now. "Lady — Sweet lady — Sweet lady of sorrow, sweet Mother of Love."

They sat listening, mesmerized. His eyes opened, and locked into hers; and he addressed her directly, in a conversational tone.

"Miss — it's not *outside* where you'll find him," (and his voice seemed to echo: find him, find *him*). "It's not out on the streets, it's not out in the fields. It's in *here*," he said, placing his hand gently and reverently upon his own heart.

Joey was mute with astonishment; but the woman — it was as if a fog had lifted from her mind. The mists evaporated from her voice, and she spoke in a clear-headed tone.

"You are right. I had to hear that. I can't spend the rest of my life grieving for my fiancé. It's been fifteen years since he walked out on me, fifteen since he married her instead. It's time for me to get over him, and get on with my life."

She thanked them and turned to leave, then paused briefly in the doorway, gesturing with the clip of her purse.

Murphy waved the suggestion away.

When she was gone, Joey didn't know whether to explode, that Murphy had just blown off another client, but mostly he was plain baffled.

"Jeez, Murphy, what was *that* about? Some kinda Buddhist thing?"

A sad smile. "No, Joey; not really."

"And — *Murphy*. Just in and gone, in and gone! We never even learned the dame's name!"

Again he waved the objection aside. "Who, Miss Mysterious? Doesn't matter. With any luck her last name will be different before too long anyhow."

And then he reached around and pulled out the wad of stuff from his back trouser pocket. He surveyed it a moment, then slowly put each item aside. Two kleenex, one used and one good as new; a news clipping, from before the war; a baseball card, for a player never made the majors; a voucher that used to be good for ten cents off ... and finally The Certificate, now imprinted with an official-looking circular seal, the result of having been pressed atop an old foil containing a condom.

Murphy considered a while; then with a soft smile and a slight sigh, tore the thing slowly in half.

And that was that.

~ *The End* ~

MURPHY ON VEGETARIANISM

"No, thanks," she said. "Just a salad. — You see, I'm a vegetarian."

"Really!" said Murphy. "Y'know — I used to be a vegetarian too!"

"You *didn't*!" she exclaimed. "I ... wouldn't have imagined it, to look at you." Murphy's t-shirt bore a cartoon of a hip hamburger and hotdog doing the "Keep On Trucking" walk. "When was that?"

"Umm ... While ago ..."

"How long were you a vegetarian?"

"Mmmwell, actually ... less than a day. Sort of between breakfast and dinner. I once had a lunch with no hamburger — it was a religious thing."

The woman seemed less than impressed.

"No, I admit it," Murphy admitted, giving up hope of impressing her with his brief fling with Buddhism. "I like my steak and I like it rare. But really — you vegetarians are something genuinely special; I mean, in the scheme of things. Cause like, when a cow sees a Hindoo, he thinks, "What, me worry?" And when a pig sees a Jew, he thinks: "*I'm* cool." But *every other animal* is like *terrified* of these guys. I mean, the rabbit's thinking, "Do Jews eat rabbits?" The hamsters are wondering, "Do Muslims eat hamsters?" Heck, even the porcupine has got to ask himself, "Do Christians eat — Well, heck, Christians will eat *anything*, long's it got ketchup on it. So all these people walk through the world spreading terror on every side. They're like Attila the Hun, maybe worse. But a vegetarian — when a vegetarian walks by, all the animals in the forest breathe a sigh of relief. They probably even murmur little blessings at you. To them, you're like St. Francis."

To Murphy's surprise, the woman seemed genuinely touched. "I'd ... never looked at it that way. I'm surprised you haven't converted *yourself*."

Murphy shrugged. "I'm a fallen man."

MURPHY ON HINDUISM

"Hindu? Hm. Don't know much about it. I mean —
I know, it's somewhere over yonder ... " He waves his
hand vaguely towards the other side of the ocean. "And
maybe some around here as well, I don't know.
Basically I never run into 'em. They must go to
different bars.

"Anyhow, Hindus. Yeh, Hindus; hummph. Don't
know exactly what it is, but the whole thing is kind of
strange. I mean ... look at it. A guy like that eats lunch,
it's a *Hindu* eating lunch. Guy goes to a movie, it's a
Hindu at the movies. I mean ... the guy can't even take
a crap without being a *Hindu*, you know what I mean?
24/7, All Hindu — All the Time. Must get kind of
tiring."

Joey splayed his hands. "No but — Murphy — I
mean it's the same like for you. You, you're a
Christian."

Murphy looked at his brother. "I hope to God you're
right."

THANKS FOR EVERYTHING

High upon noon, the sun unblinking stands,
and sheds his rays down on the quiet street,
where, frozen in siesta, nothing stirs.
Unmoving Murphy waits behinds the blinds,
his narrowed eyes still scan the street through slits.
The whiskey in the bottle now is low,
and with the liquor ebbs his hope's last drop
that any client to him ever come,
and bow, and beg, and say: I crave a boon.

Yet hark! upon the hushed midsummer air
a click of heel on pavement hither comes,
now hurried, now hesitating if to go,
now gaining strength, and resolutely on.

Thus Murphy lifts the lit butt to his lips
and sucks a drag that fills his hungering lungs.
A hundred questions wrestle in his mind.
A dame in trouble, come to seek his aid,
or trouble itself, in lipstick and high heels?
Yet beggars no choosers be, cannot refuse
what Fate flings laughing on their empty plate.
With firm resolve he stubs the ember out,
shuts the booze drawer, in calm awaits the knock.

It comes, though softly, tentative at first,

as if not meaning it, or practicing;
then hearing no response, begins to beat
more loudly now, and with a quicker pace,
till flailing with both fists upon the oak
she sends reverberation through the room.

Squaring his shoulders, Murphy pulls the door.
A redhead on the threshold startles back,
then lowers her hands, and swiftly is blasée.
"So you're the private eye?" she says and shrugs,
looking about the room with some distaste,
its bare floor flecked with ashes and old burns,
and scattered dishes crusted in the sink.

Murphy looks too, her new gaze points afresh
to scenes grown dim to him, since over-known.
The faded paint, one square of darker hue
where once a painting hung in place, now pawned;
a calendar depicting power tools
while babes in swimsuits wield them with a grin —
he starts, to note it shows the last month's date.

To her his gaze returns: say five-foot-six,
compact of build, and nearing middle age,
the which with rouge she labors to disguise.
Her lipstick clashes with her carrot-top;
her nails are yet another shade of red.

"Yawanna stare s'more," she ups and snaps,

"or are ya gonna aks a lady in?"
He blinks and winces, wordless waves her on,
and fumbles for a smoke: he needs a friend.
She looks around as though she spots no chair;
he pulls it towards her, gestures, mumbles "Please."
She shakes her curls and sits down, ladylike.
He sits down on the keg, and smokes, and waits.

"So you're a private eye," she says again,
but this time looks him fully in the face.
He nods; what can he add; and still he waits.
"Just happens I got a little job for you.
My man run out on me — the dirty rat.
I figure you can hunt him up for me.
I'll lay a C-spot on you for your time."

To her the gumshoe: "Finding guys' my game.
But counselor I'm not; you'll have to find
a priest or shrink, like that; I'm not your man.
Suppose I find him; that won't bring him back."
To him the sheila: "No, you got it wrong.
I'm finished with the bum; good riddance, too.
But when he left, he left with every dime,
leaving me nothing; I just want what's mine.
The clincher is, he swiped my wedding ring,
just slips it off my hand while I'm asleep."

This got to Murphy; got him in his gut.
    "Of all the rotten — Yes, I'll help you out.

You'll get your ring all right, I find the guy,
and maybe pop him one; no extra charge."
She grins and toasts him with a made-up glass.
"For such an ugly mug, you're not half bad."
"Same to you, sister. So: you got a name?"
"Name's Norma. Norma Rand. My husband's
Frank.
And here's his picture, so's you'll know him when."
He studies it: by looks, a decent guy.
But then, you never know. "So tell me, Norm',
how long's it been since he has left your bed?"
"Three weeks today, the bastard ups and splits.
Never a phone call, never a note good-bye.
And me with nothing to eat or pay the rent."
"Oh man, oh man," says Murph, "it takes all kinds.
I'd like to find the guy for you for free,
except I'm owing at the package store.
So tell me anyhow what-all you know —
his habits, haunts, his friends, just any leads
I'll need if I'm to find him where he's hid."

Her chin comes up, she gets an airy tone.
"Well, that's not hard, he's at the Lucky Dime.
A dive on Walnut, where he spends his time."
Now Murphy blinks his eyes; this don't compute.
"You know where Frank is — what you need me
for?"
She shakes her head, annoyed. "I go alone,
he blows me off, then I don't get what's mine."

"Yeh, well ... makes sense ... okay, let's hit the road."
They leave. He shuts the door, but doesn't lock;
nothing to steal; nothing that's worth a damn.

They drive in silence, down the empty streets.
Some things he wonders: How did it go wrong?
When fell you out of love — or never in?
But Murphy, him, he never had a dame
to call his own; and Norma still is hitched.
He just can't ask her things; cannot presume.
He takes it slow, driving as though his life
depended on her safety in his hands.

He spots the neon of the Lucky Dime,
winking now on, now off, now on again.
He parks and climbs out; halts, and goes around,
then opens the door for Norma to get down,
standing mute embarrassed as she does.
They walk on in, and grab an empty booth
halfway between the pool-hall and the bar.
She hoists her hand and waves the barkeep over.
"What's yours?" she asks; and Murphy licks his
teeth,
sensing the taste of what he cannot have.
"Rye whiskey, straight; but never on the job."
She shrugs, and asks the usual for herself.
The barkeep nods, goes off, and soon is back.
"Enjoy it, Norma," setting a bourbon down.

Now Murphy in his mind is getting strange.
"What — " "Shh. Back there." She points towards a
door
beyond the hall, with beads the doorway hung.
She beckons, and he follows her on down.
They peer between the beads; he sees a man,
Frank's very spit and image, at his cards,
betting and laughing with a bunch of friends.
Then Murphy sets his jaw; — but all at once
lashing like lightning, Norma sends a lamp
go smashing with a crash against the wall.
And lo — she throws her drink down Murphy's
shirt,
then grabs him by the ears and pulls him down
on top of her, careening back they fall
across a table, where she holds him tight.

The sound of chairs pushed back; confused alarm;
the beads are thrust aside and Frank storms out.
"What gives?!" He freezes. Norma calls out "Help!"
then thrusting with her arms, dumps Murphy off.
He's big, is Frank, more than the photo showed,
and now he stands surrounded by his pals.
Murphy just sits and stares, too dazed to move.
"Who's this?" barks Frank, and jerks an angry
thumb.
But Norma twists and smiles, not angry now.
"Just some shmuck, Frank, but then he cut up
rough.

You're gone three days; I need a little fun."
He glares at Murphy, yet seems not too keen
that anyone but Norma fill his gaze.
"I'm sorry, babe, I know I let you down.
It's just sometimes I got to soothe my nerves
with whiskey and a friendly poker game.
I'm winning, too — I meant to get the dough
to buy you that red dress you're hankering for."
She smiles and bats her lashes, downcast eyes.
Then Frank chokes as he notices her hands.
"Babe — Norma, honey, baby — where's your ring?"
"Heck Frank, right here, I put it in my bag.
I reckon you're no proper husband, so ..."
"I'll see to that!" he cries, then Murphy grabs.
"Here's this, you bum, for nosin' round my wife!"
He sends a crashing fist, and Murphy falls.
"Still my big man," she flirts, and gives her arm.
He slips the ring on; lo, and they are gone.

*

That night, in his familiar neighborhood,
out on the sidewalk, Murphy sits alone.
Baffled, and too broke to buy a drink.
He stares up through the smog to spot the stars.

Then in the hushful dark, he hears a van
draw up from nowhere, sees a form emerge,
a black man all in white, with one gold tooth,

grinning from ear to ear, and holding forth
a glass decanter, filled with liquid gold,
accents of amber, glowing with inner fire.
"Here, boss," he tips his cap, and vanishes
into the van, drives off, and soon is gone.
A shot-glass, too, upon the silver tray,
and ice in silver bucket, thick with dew.

So to the skies now Murphy hoists a toast,
knowing he is forgiven, as he forgives,
speaking a blessing, even as he is blest.

~ *The End* ~

UPCOMING MURPHY NOVELS

Following are the first chapters of soon to be released complete novels featuring the Murphy Brothers.

1) Murphy on the Mount

2) Murphy Get Your Gun

MURPHY ON THE MOUNT

CHAPTER ONE

So one June, one afternoon, we're sitting around and I say: "You know what I think, Joey?"

"What do you think Murphy?"

"I think we need a secretary."

He looks at me like my strait-jacket's slipped, he's thinking I bust outa my bin. "A *secretary*? Murphy we got no *customers*, whadawe need a secretary for?"

"You know, some slick broad, class up the front office, handle our calls."

"Murphy Murphy, nobody *calls* us. The front office, that's just the front a *this* office, the place where the beds fold up durina day. We don't got but one room!"

"Not counting the pool room," I astutely note.

"Dang right I'm not countina pool room, whacha gonna do, yagonna put 'er in *there*? In back? Plus first you know you'd hafta move out that moose head, Murphy — "

"Oh don't get on to me about that moose head again."

"An 'en all them *pizza* boxes, all piled up, like it's a tower to heaven — "

"It is, it is! 'Smatta wichoo, you never played with blocks?"

"An 'en-a *tires*, Murphy, o-o-o-o-o-oh, the tires ..."

"Yeh well you know how it is."

"That I do, Murphy, that I do. Other guys pick up stray cats or stray diseases, you you pick up stray tires."

"You know it, Joey. Tires what had no home."

"I know, I know it, Murphy. I'm not knocking your tires."

"They're nice tires."

"The best — in their day. But just — *Mu-u-ur-r*-phy..."

And right then — bingo — a knock at the door.

"Now see what I mean, Joey? A customer! Don't you wish we had a secretary right now? She could deal with 'em while we hide in back, say we're too busy, say that we died."

"C'mon, Murphy, party's gonna get tired knocking. Opena door."

"You open it. Makes me nervous, customers."

Joey opens it and, Ooh Wah Doo, a customer, and what a customer! It's a dame, but that don't describe it. I mean, your mother's a dame, if it comes to that. No I mean like a, *da-a-ame* dame: with everything on it. She got shiny hair so clear you could shave your face in it. She got lips like a paint sale. She got teeth, make a dentist say: I'm ready, Lord, I seen it all, you can take me now. She got eyes like ice, and it's not melting. A neck, would make the Boston Strangler just throw up his hands, he wouldn't hardly know where to begin. Then a blouse, a white blouse, the front part of it all scooped out, like a dish of ice cream. And below, oh, the double dip, I'm peeking through my fingers; and her waist is like a sugar cone. Then all that flesh that was left over from the middle, they just slabbed it on the hips with a trowel. And then she goes and tapers down again, she's like a spinning top, you'd a think she'd fall over, just these slim little feet and tall high heels and the shoes come to a point like a kick-knife.

"You a shamus?" she says, looking at Joey. He blushes and mumbles, "Me an' him."

She looks me over, half her mouth does this little stab at a smile. "You'll do." And I think: You too.

I tip the beer-cans off the chair and offer it to her like a gentleman. With a ladylike swish, she sits down. I sit down on the crate, and Joey sort of edges off to the kitchen part of the room.

"I got a job for you," she says.

"Well we're pretty busy, but I guess I can fit in you, I mean fit you in."

I think I maybe I see an eyebrow move, but not much. "*You* ? — b-*busy*??!!" she says. — I don't like the tone.

I match it. "Yeh, we was thinkina doin' our nails."

Definitely a budge of an eyebrow this time. I think.

"It's like this, shamus. There's a fellow that I want to see him dead."

Oh no not again. I sort of get off the crate real slow. "Listen, sister, maybe we're hungry but we're not *that* hungry. We'd be eating the last little leavings outa the garbage can what the *wino* left behind, and we still not be up for *that*. You come to the wrong address."

"Can it, shamus. There's just a guy that I want you to find him, is all — dead or alive, though dead would suit me just dandy."

"Hm, well, we usually like our clients alive."

She glares at me and snaps: "*He's* not your client — *I* am!"

Joey and I make these little O's with our mouths and look at each other and shake our heads.

"Well now that remains to be seen, and me I'm not seein' it," I say, "'cause you was just leavin'."

"Yeh," says Joey, opening the door, "we're real sorry you coulden stay."

She stands up fast, eyes sending out sparks, kind of quivering, but then — some little tendon somewhere snaps, she starts twisting her handbag, and the ice in her eyes turns to slush. "I'm — sorry. I snapped at you. If you'll hear me out, you'll see why I'm so tense."

Again the glance-exchange with Joey but this time no O's.

"An apology!" I comment.

He nods concurrence. "An actual apology."

"That magic word 'sorry' that makes things all better. — Okay, sister, take a seat, I reckon you can find it yourself this time."

She found it all right.

"So okay, so how's about you tell us in your own words what happen. Who is this guy?"

"My husband — my *ex*, if I have anything to do with it."

Dang. "Lady — really sorry — we don't do divorce cases."

Impatient. "He walked out on me. Not much left to divorce. Just hear me out, okay? Later for the scruples."

"All right. And how'd you meet this guy, when he was still your *to-be*?"

"I was working in a travel agency at the time — Willie's Worldwide Travel, downtown. Richie was a steady customer, always flying off to places like Zurich, the Cayman Islands, Rome, Naples, Corsica — really sent me back to the geography books sometimes. I didn't fall so much in love with *him* as with the places he was always going to — not even the places, really, since I never seen a one of them, but just like the idea of the places, the *names*."

We maintained a respectful silence, and she went on.

"Willie my boss was a prize flagpole. All day yakking on the phone, not work stuff either, stuff with his hobby, which was breeding dogs. Like we don't already got enough dogs. Never did a lick of work otherwise. But he knew people, they came in. I think he knew Richie from before. But they weren't close — he still let me handle Ritchie's reservations. And what reservations — first class all the way.

"Me I'm just the girl here, you know, but one time, it's about the tenth time I'm making him a reservation, and I been learning about his tastes and all, what he chooses in a hotel, and ecsetera like that. And now Willie's out somewhere and I'm alone with him in the office, so I ask him, flirting a little, is it business or pleasure. And he gives me this — *dreamy* smile, I mean not like he was dreaming but just this soft shy elegant dignified hint of a smile, and murmurs: 'A little of both.'

"That did it for me. I must of blushed. Anyway he laughed and said, 'You're quite a girl.' And I said, 'I am?', and the sunlight's streaking in through the little windows that they could use some washing and bouncing off his gold watch and it's like the brightest object in the room. Then he says, 'And it might be a pleasure, doing business with you.' Now normally I don't allow a gentleman says something like that to me, but he gives this big smile and his teeth are *perfect* and I'm thinking, This can't be happening to me. He's obviously loaded, always pays cash, just peeling off these crisp hundred-dollar bills from a wad as big and round as a, as I don't know what. 'Yes', he says, 'You are quite — a — gal ... ' And I sigh and I say, 'Do you really think so?', not even caring am I being too forward for a nice girl because at this point I am willing to risk all — "

"Hey, could we cut to the chase a little?" breaks in Joey. "Save that for the weepie magazines. I think I'm gonna lose my lunch."

"*Anyway*," glaring, "he asks me out, says we'll have dinner in Paris and do I have any favorite places there, well I quit my job right then and there, leaving a nasty note for Willie on his computer screen and go out flipping the sign around so it says 'Sorry We Missed You — CLOSED'. Then, well, something comes up and we don't go to Paris, but we go to my apartment, and you can guess the rest. And then I'm crying, and he's laughing and stroking my hair, and calling me 'Silly thing' but in a nice way, and it's getting to me, yes, it's getting to me, and I put my arms around him and I draw him down to me, and he asks, Will you marry me?, and I say Yes, I say Yes — yes — yes yes yes yes yes."

"'Yes'; right. We heard you the first time."

"We just go and get married quick at the registry because he has this incredibly important business trip, he's gonna buy us a house with what he makes on it, but he promises a round-the-world honeymoon soon — *not* through Willie's Worldwide," a bitter smile, "and then house-hunting."

"And then maybe you got time, you get married the right way," says Joey grimly. "In a church."

She doesn't notice. "He says he wants to keep me in style — in a style I'm unaccustomed to — and I shall never want for anything." Even with all that later happened, she sighs at the memory.

"Guess you had ta be there," Joey mutters.

"He says we should have a joint bank account — share and share alike! Only his is so large he can't move it over without interest penalties and things, so instead we add his name to mine. I've been tucking away what I can, living pretty simply so it's finally come up to something, and he's going to add to it out of the profits of his trip, soon's he gets back. And I say Darling, you are too good to me, and I embrace him around the neck — "

Joey starts leafing through a magazine.

" — and he laughs and then he gets passionate again, and we have quite a time of it until alas it's time for him to leave."

I nod. Don't like where this is going.

"That was two weeks ago. A week later he's still not back, and then I get a notice from my bank that my check has bounced. A five-dollar check! So I go in to see what is this, and they tell me my account has been cleaned out, what, didn't I know; just only not closed out, because that requires both signatures. Then I go back to my apartment and some other things are missing, things I'm really gonna miss, and I realize I've been had. And had good."

Nodding, frowning. "So you come straight to us."

"Not right away. I still can't believe it. Some — crazy mistake, or ... I mean he never acted shifty or anything, if he's really a bad actor then he's a really good actor. But another week goes by and no call, not even a post card, so I finally say, Girl, that does it; and I come to you."

Okay; check. "So how you find out about us? Been talking to one of our many satisfied customers?"

"You were in the phone book, only listing with no ad and no bold-face or nothing, just a number and a name. So I figured you were cheap. I mean he — took everything."

"Hmm. Cheap is as cheap does. So how much you were figuring you could afford?"

"Well ... What are your usual rates?"

I look over to Joey. Gimme a figure! What do I know? But before he can say anything, she says:

"It doesn't matter anyways. Richie cleaned me out. I'll have to pay you when you find him — brother, I'll make him pay! And if he's dead, then I'll inherit, then I'll be rolling in it, and you can name your price."

"Mm. Hunh. Just a moment while I consult with my colleague."

We step back into the pool room and close the door.

"This is worse than Wimpy," says Joey. "'I will gladly pay you Tuesday for a hamburger today', only in the meantime you have to find me the money."

"Which we are to get — "

" — from her worst enemy, a con man slippery as an eel — "

" — who's probably by now in another country — "

" — what we don't know what country it is."

"Does not look good."

"That it does not."

"Bad."

"Real bad."

"But on the other hand — "

" — we know what beggars can't be."

"She's on."

"She's on."

We go back in, looking grave.

"Good news, madam. Owing to certain unusual features of interest, we have decided to take your case."

Murphy Get Your Gun

The sign on the glass part of the door says, or said, "Murphy Bros., Private Investigators"; and then in smaller letters, "Discretion Assured." Fancy glass, frosted. The words part, some of it's flaked and some of it's faded, but parts of it are real good.

Bros., meaning Brothers, that'd be Joey. My little brother what's bigger than me. You mess with me, you gotta mess with my brother. And vice versa, of course.

The office is way at the back, one flight up, and none of the other rooms is rented. Downstairs it's a bodega, only closed; used to be a pizzeria. Used to be a candy store before that. We seen 'em come and we seen 'em go, lemme tell ya. But us, things stay about the same. Joey says maybe we oughta advertise but me I say, Naw, the best guys go by word of mouth.

So we don't get a lot of customers but we stay in business, no problem. Still in business, maybe business is slow. Two can live cheaper than one and all that plus a little here, a little there, we get by. You might say we're independently needy.

This gives us a lot of time to shoot pool in the little room behind our living space that doubles as an office, and that's like I like it. Real swell table, courtesy of a previous dead tenant.

So Tuesday, we're shooting eight-ball, and me I'm going after the striped guys. And I'm going great, pock pock pock, rightina pocket, it's like they're down in order and — and then, and then this jane walks in and throws me off my game. She'd knocked on the outer door, she says, which was anyhow open; no reply so she walked back to where the sounds were coming from. So me I get hot under the collar, I mean I'm *on* my *game* here, and I ignore her, but him, old Joey can be gentle, you ought to see him, he's like a big moose. He just motions her into the office with a little sad smile like he's a clergyman or an undertaker and I give up and follow them in.

She's about forty, used to be pretty. Little kind of a hat thing perched up on top. Teeny old-fashion handbag and a little flower handkerchief that she's twisting it. She's not saying anything and Joey says, real gentle: You can tell us.

She bites her lip and I'm still thinking of that pool game and suddenly I think I know a beautiful shot, not the obvious one. I just wanta hop in next door, just for a sec, check out the angles, but then the customer starts talking and Joey gives me this kind of look. She says her husband is disappeared.

Oh right, we hadda stop a pool game for *this*? Disappeared, huh, *disappeared*, right, just that that, a man disappears — you expect us to believe that? Right in a puff a smoke right? Tell me another one that's just is good!

Now it's not nice policy to yell at customers even when they're loony, customer is always right and ecsetera and all that. But gimme a break. Cos like I said, I was hot under the collar and here's this *dame* is coming up here for no good reason and queering my game. I can feel my winning streak just draining away like beer down a bathtub.

And then she does something that dames do, it's their secret weapon: she starts to cry. Whimper whimper whimper, dab dab dab with the hankie, I mean gimmeabreak. Joey says Excuse us I got to consult with Dr. Murphy, and he leads me back into the pool room and closes the door. Me I start checking out the lay of the table but he jerks my face around and says You're the smart one so how's about you wise up. Okay okay, ya don't hafta get sore.

So we go back in to the client and I say I have consulted with my associate and, sure enough, there was a case like that, back in '47, very unusual, guy just disappeared. So we're sorry we didn't buy your story but now we do.

So okay. What time did he pull his disappearing act? — Last Tuesday, that'd be March 31, middle of the afternoon. It had been exactly a week. — So why didn't you come to us sooner? (Showing concern.) — She figured he might come back. (Good answer.) — And

what were the circumstances of him disappearing? —
There was no circumstances. He's just watching TV and
she goes out to the store for some sausages and when
she gets back he's not there. No note, no nothing. Cops
all over the place a coupla doors down; who knows,
some incident; but nobody saw nothing, knows
nothing, zip.

Oh that's just great, that's real super. Smoke would
of been better cause at least that might of been a gun.
So I say and what's a citizen doing watching TV on a
Tuesday afternoon while the rest of us taxpayers are
slaving away? I hold up my hands, with the pool-cue
calluses. She says he's retired, on disability, just turn
sixty in the fall. Now then I start putting two and two
together, like I said I'm the brains of the outfit, and I
ask what was she planning on being her method of
preferred payment for our little fee — cash on the
barrelhead or not at all? She shrugs, says there's no
particular problem with that, and she pulls out a small
roll of small bills. So we're friends again.

Already two scenarios look ruled out. They have
some money, live simple, he's not skipping out on
debts. And he's sixty. Now, the wife turns forty, the
guy's about forty-five, he's still got all his juices and he
wants to check out the action somewhere else. 'S
natural he disappears, what's the mystery? But sixty,
and forty, and him on disability — it doesn't figure.
Maybe, but not as likely. I ask her delicate as I can if
their relations were, well, you know, okay and

everything. She doesn't seem to be shucking when she says they were still very much in love.

I get kinda touched by that, I'm liking her better — bygones be bygones on that pool game, not her fault. You can still see where she mighta been a knockout, back in the day; and that's probably what the guy still sees, seeing her now and thinking back. — How long they been married? — "Twenty-three years." — Twenty, three, *years*!

Yeh we'll help this babe. The setup sounds all right.

APOLOGIA PRO AMICO SUO

He's a good sort, all told; great guy to have a brew with; but some have remarked, that he does sometimes cut up rough. In addition, Murphy occasionally permits himself a word or two which, at the time these stories are more or less set (Truman and Eisenhower eras), were in quite general use among the working population, yet which, in latter days, have fallen out of favor with the politer circles at Bryn Mawr. In the face of such grave criticisms, we can only observe, that he is compact of contradictions like any Postlapsarian Man.

There was the time, to take just one, when he saved a child from a burning building. True, he simply happened to be lounging nearby on the sidewalk, leaning against a fire hydrant and sucking down the delicious, soothing smoke that comes from the unique blend of domestic and Turkish tobaccos in the original, unfiltered Camel, filling the lungs to the brim with joy and gladness, lightening the intellect and sharpening his already keen observational skills, when he noticed that a fire had broken out; and true, he went in partly out of idle curiosity; still, he did toss aside (safely into a puddle) a perfectly good and only half-smoked butt, which in less urgent circumstances might well have been gently extinguished and set aside for his after-supper repast; and when he happened upon the kid, engrossed in a comic and oblivious to the gathering peril, he did do the decent thing and shoo the urchin out the door. And yet, not three days after this act of chivalry, he was discovered dead drunk in a bordello down on South Street.

Nothing in his life became him like the living it — to the hilt, with all its faults. With all that, it is our fondest hope, and most cherished belief, that despite all buffets, of Time and the Devil, our dear friend Murphy may yet one day be saved.